PENGUIN BOOKS
HEAR THE WIND BLOW, DEAR

David M. Pierce was born in Montreal, Canada. He lived for some years in London, where, among other things, he wrote songs for the pop group *Meal Ticket* and acted in a Shakespearian theatre group. He co-authored a musical with fellow Canadian Rick Jones and has written songs with Jeremy Clyde. His other publications include three volumes of verse and a cookery book, written with singer Annie Ross. He has written two other books featuring private investigator Vic Daniel, *Roses Love Sunshine* and *Down in the Valley*, both published by Penguin.

DAVID M. PIERCE

HEAR THE WIND BLOW,
DEAR

PENGUIN BOOKS

PENGUIN BOOKS

Published by the Penguin Group
27 Wrights Lane, London W8 5TZ, England
Viking Penguin Inc., 40 West 23rd Street, New York, New York 10010, USA
Penguin Books Australia Ltd, Ringwood, Victoria, Australia
Penguin Books Canada Ltd, 2801 John Street, Markham, Ontario, Canada L3R 1B4
Penguin Books (NZ) Ltd, 182–190 Wairau Road, Auckland 10, New Zealand

Penguin Books Ltd, Registered Offices: Harmondsworth, Middlesex, England

First published 1989
1 3 5 7 9 10 8 6 4 2

Copyright © David M. Pierce, 1989
All rights reserved

Made and printed in Great Britain by
Richard Clay Ltd, Bungay, Suffolk
Filmset in Monophoto Sabon

For Aneta

I invented many things herein –
including all of the people – but not
Los Angeles or the San Fernando
Valley. It is not known who
invented them.

CHAPTER ONE

Bitten by a llama.

It wasn't fair.

Things were going to be different. After all, it was a new year – 1985.

I was upwardly mobile. I had just talked my landlady into replacing all the carpets in our apartment. I had a new air-conditioning unit in my office that only made as much noise as Niagara Falls during the spring floods. Yet, undeniably, there I was, being bitten by a llama, a mother llama.

I made a noise of some kind. One might call it a scream. The young girl next to me who was holding the mother llama's smelly baby also made a noise, a sort of choking in the throat, the type of strangled sound unfeeling women make when they are unsuccessfully trying to stifle laughter. I gave her a bitter glance.

'I'm real sorry,' she said. 'Woolly's never bitten anyone before.'

'And I have never been bitten by a woolly before,' I said. 'Maybe between us Woolly and I have broken new frontiers. Perhaps I should get off a telegram to the *Guinness Book of Records* immediately.' This time the thoughtless adolescent laughed out loud.

'Here, I'll take her,' she said.

'Better late than never,' I said. The girl took Woolly's halter from me and led the animals off toward their stall while I inspected my llama-bitten arm, my pitching arm, too. I must admit that the skin wasn't broken, just gnawed a bit, thank God, because who knows what loathsome diseases llamas carry in their receding gums, elephantiasis is probably the good news, but still, it did hurt.

I stepped outside of the roofed area into the paddock or whatever the yokels call it. It was a typical January day in Southern California, temperature in the middle sixties, breezy, with a chance of rain. I was in the animal enclosure at Wonderland Park, which is an entertainment complex mainly for children about twenty-eight miles north-east of Los Angeles, off the old Interstate 8. The park was approximately one third man-eating animals and two thirds mock Tudor Village. One of its more famous features was a large waterfall, under which, when I'd arrived about a half hour earlier, I'd seen a hapless actor soaked to the skin attempting to get out his lines for some cut-rate commercial, no doubt non-union, they were shooting. Actors – didn't someone once call them poor, benighted heathens? More than likely someone married to one.

I was in the animal enclosure in the first place because of a phone call I'd gotten at the office late that morning from Woolly's keeper, the lady with the perverse sense of humor, as if there were any other kind. She wanted to know if I knew someone called Emile Douglas. I thought for a moment, then admitted I did. Emile Douglas had a run-down orchard and an assortment of goats, sheep and dogs out near Magic Mountain, one of Wonderland Park's rivals, and he spent most of his time talking to God.

'But don't think I'm nuts,' he'd say. 'If I ever hear God talking back, that'll be nuts.' I'd helped him out once and in gratitude he let me use a gulch down by his creek as a shooting range. I suppose I got in some practice out there once every six weeks or so.

It turned out that Woolly's babysitter, name of Olivia Elliot, recent graduate in veterinary medicine from the University of Cal–Davis, knew Emile as well. Wonderland Park, through her, bought the occasional goat from him, she told

2

me. And she had found out from him that I was the type of investigator whose rates were somewhere between reasonable and laughable. And she sort of needed an investigator, she said.

'What do you sort of need investigating?' I asked her over my almost-new red touchdial phone.

'It sounds real silly, I know,' she said, 'but someone's been stealing my sheep.'

'I'd look for the nearest cattle rancher if I was you, marm,' I said. 'You know how they feel about them low-down, grass-eatin', smelly critters.'

She sighed. 'I told you it'd sound silly. Listen. I run one of the animal enclosures at Wonderland Park. I'm responsible for, right now, forty-two Suffolks, six Jacobs, a herd of twenty-three goats, two llamas and a Holstein calf. I should be responsible for forty-seven Suffolks. Forty-two from forty-seven leaves five. Whether you think it's funny or not, I'm missing five sheep.'

'Who's your head of security out there?' I asked her.

'Mr Gould,' she said.

'Why don't you go to him?'

'First of all because he broke his leg on the Monster, second of all because he's in the hospital, and third of all if I did he'd probably have a fit and then fire me, if he didn't get me arrested. They've had so many problems here over the years with having stuff stolen, mainly by part-time staff, that now we gotta make good any losses in our departments, or else.'

'O K, I'll take your word for it,' I said. 'By the way, what is the Monster?'

'Are you kidding?' she said. 'It's only the world's second-largest roller coaster. It does two full upside-down circles.'

'Oh,' I said. 'Sounds like my kind of fun.'

'I didn't know what to do,' Olivia said. 'Emile told me one time about you and how you got that property guy off his back so I got your number from him. So what do you think?'

I said, 'Hang on a minute,' switched on Betsy, my Apple II computer, and checked my schedule for the day. Aside from 'Buy olives' and 'Pick up Mom's cleaning', it was blank as a fat girl's dance card.

'Are you open today?'

'Every day, rain or shine,' she said.

'What's it doing today out there?'

'Raining and shining,' she said.

'What's a good time for you?'

'About two,' she said. 'After the feeding.'

Then she told me the best way to get out there, then we had a short but amicable discussion of fees, then I said, 'See you soon,' and hung up. Then I says to myself, pard, time to saddle up an' raise some dust.

It was then about twelve thirty so I put Betsy and all my other valuables including the phone away in the mammoth safe in the washroom at the back, tidied up, then shut up shop.

At that time my office was on the corner of Victory and Orange, in the San Fernando Valley, just over the hill via Laurel Canyon Drive from wonderful West Hollywood, which was then in the process of becoming the world's first legally gay incorporated city, and when I say gay I don't mean festive. My office was one of the little group of six properties in an L-shaped mall; taken in order there was a vacant lot, then me, then the Nus' Vietnamese take-out, then their cousin's video rental, then a Taco-Burger franchise, then the Armenian shoe-repair establishment of Mr Amoyan. It was the big time at last.

After locking up, I strolled the three blocks up Victory to the local Ralph's supermarket, gave a panhandler lounging near the entrance a Canadian quarter, and went in. I didn't see my occasional drinking buddy Bill, who worked there as master butcher, so I rang the bell marked 'Attendant' that hung over one of the meat freezers. After a minute Bill came

4

out carrying a stack of plastic-wrapped T-bones which he dealt neatly into a display counter. Then he said to me, 'You rang, sir?'

'I rang,' I said. 'So how's it going?'

He shrugged and wiped his hands off on his long white apron.

'Don't ask me,' he said. 'What's up with you?'

'I'm hot on the job,' I said. 'Listen, Bill, what does a sheep cost, I mean a whole sheep, a carcass, the kind that comes to you frozen and then you cut it up and then I buy expensive pieces of?'

'Jeepers,' said Bill. 'It's got to depend on the grade, the age, where it's from, how many we buy, does it come from one of our own farms and a couple of other details I won't bother to bother you with.'

'Yeah, well, roughly,' I said.

'Well, roughly, I'd expect to pay something like fifty-five dollars for a forty-pound carcass.'

'Say a guy came to the back door and said, "Hey, Bill, I got a nice clean sheep you can have for twenty-five bucks," would you be interested?'

'Are you crazy?' Bill said. 'If it don't got the stamp, Ralph's don't want it. Me neither. To save what, a few bucks? Worse than that, I can think of at least nine fairly common diseases sheep can have and if they've got one of them you don't want to eat it. Not a chance. All right. Some two-bit little backdoor operator in East LA, what does he care how many people he kills, but still . . .' He shook his head so hard his wire-rims almost fell off.

'We drinking tonight?'

'Maybe,' I said. Even if I wasn't, Bill would be. He was a man who liked his beer. Once in a while the time I shopped at Ralph's coincided with the time Bill finished working, that would be about three thirty, and he'd give me a lift in his van to the Corner Bar, which was all of two blocks away, say a three-minute ride if you missed the lights, and he'd always crack open two large tins of Miller from the van's cooler for the drive.

I took my leave of Bill and took off down Victory toward the freeway. While I was waiting for the lights to change at Orange I saw a sign, hand-lettered on cardboard, that read, 'Carlos – the King O' Sheepskins – 30 percent off! First Left!' So instead of continuing the way I was going I took the first left and pulled in to the forecourt of an abandoned gas station where some local entrepreneurs had set up shop. There was an Asian lady selling luggage of all shapes and colors, a hopeful type peddling newly made, wooden framed mirrors with old-style ads etched on them, a market gardener working out of the back of his truck, and a sharp-looking Mexican youth selling white and black fitted sheepskin car-seat covers. Ah ha, I said to myself. Eureka. Sheeps have other assets besides their chops.

Once the Latino got over his not unfounded suspicions that I was either working for the Department of Immigration or the Internal Revenue, which he only did when I revealed to him somewhat shamefacedly what my real interest was, he became helpfulness itself. Generally speaking, he said, you could count on the skin of a standard brand being roughly the same value as the meat. He didn't know what a Jacob was but a Suffolk was white with a black face and black legs. And a Mate was all black with no horns. Was I interested in the shearing process? I wasn't particularly, I told him truthfully. I thanked him, politely declined his offer of a once-in-a-lifetime fifty percent off for two new seat covers for my Nash Metropolitan, all work done on premises, and headed out into the traffic again.

Black sheepskin seat covers for my pink and blue Nash – maybe I'd been too hasty after all.

And maybe not.

CHAPTER TWO

And so it was that by the time I got out to Wonderland Park and Olivia Elliot's animal enclosure and had my first and last encounter with a man-eating Peruvian flea-bag, I wasn't completely ignorant about sheep. I knew at least one useful thing about them, and that was, stealing one was a hard way to make a living. I also knew they were jolly good with roast potatoes and mint sauce. However, what other reasons there might be for stealing sheep aside from hunger were for me to find out. So while Olivia was rubbing her charges down or putting their feed bags on or singing them old Incan lullabies or whatever she was doing, I tried, without much luck, to think up some.

The enclosure was near the park's northern boundary; outside the fenced-in corral there was a path, then a few trees, then a six-foot wooden fence that, as far as I could see, encircled the entire complex. The dolphinarium, the next exhibit along, was off to my left; the film crew making the ad were noisily setting up over there with much unnecessary commotion. Some Girl Friday was drying the poor actor's white suit with a portable hair-dryer, no doubt in preparation for his next soaking.

About then Olivia came back, dusting her hands vigorously. She was a short, plain girl with a tanned face and a Prince Val haircut. She was wearing short shorts, half boots and a yellow T-shirt that said, appropriately, 'Wonderland Park'. I was wearing a blue waterproof windbreaker over a basically purple Hawaiian shirt, size X L.

'Murder on the hands,' Olivia said, giving me a startlingly brilliant smile. 'I keep forgetting to wear gloves.'

'I wouldn't go near those things again without full-length armor,' I said. 'Listen. Does anyone live here, or do you all go home at night?'

'About six of us live in,' she said. 'In a row of little cottages behind the admin building.' She waved vaguely in the direction away from the outer fence.

'Who?'

'Well, me, Betty, she looks after the dolphins, Tim, he looks after the bears, Fran, she's primates, there's the night watchman and his wife Susie who's one of the staff cooks and there's Mr Koven, he's sort of a general handyman and is always here in case something goes wrong with the water supply or there's a power failure or like that. And Mr Gould.'

'Who unfortunately broke his leg on the Monster,' I said. 'I don't suppose there's anywhere a guy could buy a girl a beer around here.'

'Are you totally insane?' she said. 'One drink here and you are out. We can get a Coke through there.' She pointed at a refreshment stand just visible through the trees.

'Lead the way.'

As we were walking along the path towards the stand, which I could see by then was called Ye Cat 'n' Fiddle, I asked her when the thefts had started.

'Gee, I know when I first noticed for sure,' she said, kicking a pebble a mile. 'I sort of noticed I hadn't seen Muffy for a while but it didn't really sink in that she wasn't there until I couldn't find Fat Ass one day.'

'Fat Ass?' I said, raising my brows. 'Really, Olivia, you shock me.'

'I'll bet,' she said, grinning up at me from under her heavy bangs.

'Do all the animals have names?' I kicked at a pine cone and just missed it.

'Oh, some of them,' she said. 'I named Fat Ass after Mr Gould.'

'And when was this?'

'Two days ago,' she said. 'As for when it started, I can't be sure but it can't be more than a couple of weeks.'

'One more thing of vital importance,' I said. 'What's a Jacob?'

'White,' she said. 'With dark brown spots. Sometimes they have four horns.'

'Better them than me,' I said.

We got to the stand and perched ourselves on a couple of stools at one end. A pretty girl in a more or less, mostly less, Elizabethan outfit complete with lace cap who Olivia called Piggy took our orders for two Cokes, got them, served them with a mock curtsey, then went back to puzzling over some cards that looked like stock sheets. A minute later I heard her mutter a couple of words that certainly weren't in Shakespeare.

We sipped our Cokes in silence for a while, then Olivia turned to me and asked, 'Now what, Mr Daniel? Any thoughts on the subject?'

I was watching a family that was strolling, or rather, waddling by – overweight mother in shorts and flip-flops, beer-bellied father in shorts and undershirt, fat child in shorts and obviously new yellow 'Wonderland Park' T-shirt a size too small, all three of them eating from large boxes of candy-covered popcorn.

'My thoughts are that a family that stuffs itself together gets fat together,' I said. 'About the sheep. On the way here I talked to Bill the master butcher and Carlos the sheepskin king. From what they told me I don't think anyone is stealing your sheep for the money.'

'Me neither,' Olivia said. 'I just have a feeling it isn't that easy.'

'You say there's no drinking here, at all?'

'Uh uh,' she said. 'We go into town.'

'You also said there are no bored, part-time workers living

in, like college kids, because bored college kids and drinking can often, if not usually, lead to excruciatingly funny behavior like filling up convertibles with water, throwing people off balconies into swimming pools, panty raids, and who knows, hiding sheep in someone's clothes cupboard.'

'No way,' Olivia said, slurping the last of her Coke. I gave her a friendly slurp right back.

'Where that leaves us I don't quite know. Let me think for a minute.'

'Be my guest,' she said.

'How about during the day?' I said after a bit. From the distance I could hear screams as the Monster passed by.

'How?' she asked.

'How should I know,' I said. 'In a truck?'

'No way,' she said. 'I'm here all day and every day. I have to let some of the animals out every hour for the kids to play with and I have to watch them every second so they don't get hurt.'

'The kids?'

'The animals,' she said. 'Who cares about the kids?'

I paid Piggy for the Cokes and we headed back to the sheep pens.

'I'm going to have a look around,' I told her. 'After I do so outside, can you drive everyone out so I can have a look around inside?'

'Why not?' she said. She took a look at her watch. 'Oops. Feeding time.'

'Who gets fed?'

'Elmer,' she said.

'Elmer who?'

'Elmer, my calf,' she said proudly. 'Three weeks old today.'

'Oh, darn,' I said. 'And I forgot to get a card.' She grinned again and went off to give Elmer his bottle.

I looked around. The ground was mostly hard-packed dirt

with the occasional scattering of fresh straw; all I could see was hundreds of hoofprints. A few spectators who were hanging over the wooden three-railed fence watched me with interest, especially when I got down on my hands and knees.

'What kind of sheep is that, Mom?' the inevitable fat kid loudly asked his mother, which raised a hearty laugh from all but me. Then I went inside and told Olivia she could start the sheep drive anytime.

She looked out the door to check that the corral gate hadn't been unlatched by some fun-loving visitor, then let all the animals except for Woolly and child out of their stalls, then shooed them outside. She went back for Elmer and began to bottle feed him or her or it, letting the youngest of the children take turns helping her.

Inside, I checked every inch of the floor except for the llama stall and found exactly what I had found outside – nothing but hoofprints, straw, and sheep and goat and llama shit. No blood, no bullet holes, no spent cartridge cases, no nothin'. I was not, of course, and more than likely never will be, the last of the Mohicans, but I doubt that even he could have found anything useful, such as traceable footprints, in that lot.

So now what, kemo sabe?

I went back outside, climbed the rail fence as unobtrusively as possible, and meandered down the path that ran alongside the perimeter six-foot wall – no footprints there either as the path was flagstoned. Neither were there any tufts of wool caught on handy bushes or empty mint jelly jars.

Some twenty yards along I came to a gate where a paved service road entered the park just past the dolphinarium; the gate was locked but could be unlatched from the inside without a key. So what, some may say. Outside, the service road ran off in both directions and obviously circled the whole park area. So what again.

Across the road was a two-strand barbed-wire fence and

immediately beyond that there began a hardy but stunted collection of junipers, pines and assorted other Christmas trees covering the side of a low hill. And beyond the low hill was a higher hill and beyond that a still higher one and beyond that, gray sky and dragon country. A sign nailed on one of the fence posts informed me that I was facing State of California Forestry Department land and that all access was forbidden.

I sighed, as there didn't seem to be a lot else to do at the time. I brushed some sheep shit off my tan corduroys. Then I chucked a rock at a tree trunk to see if I would ever be able to pitch in the majors again, but I missed it by a mile. I wondered if anyone had ever successfully sued a llama. Then I went back inside.

I found Olivia doing something so unpleasant to one of the sheep – a Jacob, as a matter of fact – that I'll spare you the details. I told her that I'd had an idea of sorts, and that I'd be in touch, then headed back towards the car park. I passed the Monster on the way, which looked every bit as unpleasant as I'd imagined, also the poor thespian, who was standing in his shirtsleeves looking extremely unhappy right in front of a sign that read, 'Ye Olde Bear Pit'.

I didn't see a merry-go-round. I wonder whatever happened to them. I had my first kiss on a merry-go-round, my first real kiss. I was seven at the time and still wearing breeches. She was older than me, I remember, but I can't remember her name. Men can be such brutes.

CHAPTER THREE

I didn't bother stopping off at the office on the way home but did remember to pick up Mom's drycleaning. Home at that time was the upper half of a duplex on Windsor Castle Terrace, just after the freeway overpass; it was your standard Valley two-bedroom apartment with dimpled cottage-cheese ceilings, white walls, white floor-length curtains, and, in our case, new brown wall-to-wall carpeting which Mom was busily vacuuming when I entered.

'Damn things,' she said crossly. 'All they do is shed.'

'So do llamas,' I said, giving her a pat on the head. My mom is a short, still pretty woman, seventy-one last November. I hung her cleaning – two trouser suits, one canary yellow, the other a wine color – in her cupboard, got myself a Corona from the icebox, sat down on the sofa near the phone, got up again to get the telephone book from the little table near the door, and began looking up state governmental departments. After a minute Mom kicked off the machine and wheeled it out to the kitchen. She came back in and perched on the arm of the sofa beside me.

'Working?' she asked me, reaching up to do something to what was left of my hair.

'Um hum.' I found the number I was looking for and dialed it. While it was ringing, my mom asked me again,

'Working?'

I said, 'Um-hum,' again but there must have been something in the way I said it or in my expression when I said it despite my best efforts because Mom immediately got up and took a few angry steps around the room.

'Now, now,' I said.

'Oh, shoot,' she said. 'Did I already ask you?'

'Um-hum,' I said. I got a recorded voice on the line that asked me not to hang up, my call would be answered as soon as a member of the staff was available.

'How many times?' Mom asked.

I held up two fingers. My mother had Alzheimer's disease, one of the symptoms of which is a frequent loss of memory. More often than not she laughed it off when she realized she'd asked the same question over and over because she'd forgotten she'd asked it in the first place, but occasionally she got miffed. Occasionally she cried.

'Forestry, Ms Hanson,' a girl's voice said in my ear. 'Can I help you?'

'I hope so,' I said. 'My name is Victor Daniel, and I would like to know how I find out who is in charge of a particular piece of forestry land.'

'If it is part of a National Forest,' Ms Hanson said, 'you want the Forest Service, which is under the Agriculture Department.'

'The sign said it was state owned,' I said.

'In that case,' she said, 'try me.'

'Ms Hanson,' I said, 'who is in charge of, or looks after, or caretakes, the forestry land that abuts the north side of Wonderland Park, which is about twenty-eight miles north-east of LA?'

'We do,' she said. 'In conjunction with the Sheriff's Department.'

'Ms Hanson, is there somewhere a particular person, or team, that knows that area, that actually patrols it or maintains a fire watch?'

'Sure,' she said. 'That would be out of Parson's Crossing.'

'Ah,' I said. 'And where would Parson's Crossing be, I wonder.'

She told me; I'd passed within a few miles of it twice that day, going and coming from Wonderland Park.

I thanked Ms Hanson for her help, and hung up.

'Mom, where's your beeper?' I said. Actually, I knew where it was, it was on the cocktail table in front of me, right beside the ring my cold beer was making.

'So I took it off to vacuum, big deal,' my mother said, pinning it back on her sweater. What the beeper did, when activated, was alert our downstairs neighbor and landlady, Phoebe ('Call me Feeb') that Mom needed help.

I got up and stretched, then started getting back into my windbreaker.

'Want some late lunch before you go?'

'Nah,' I said. 'I'll pick up something on the way.'

'Hot dogs,' said Mom, making a face, although she liked them as much as I did. I bent over and kissed her cheek; it was a long way down because, as I mentioned, Mom was short, about five foot two, and I was extremely large, being six foot seven and a fourth. Where the height came from, no one knew, as Pop had only been a few inches taller than Mom and none of my grandparents even close to six feet. And my brother Tony, who ran the records section for the Central Division of the LAPD, wouldn't even have been allowed to enter Mr Big, which, if you don't know, is a chain of West Coast clothing stores whose smallest size is a 42-long.

'Black is beautiful,' said some black. 'Brown is cute,' said Lee Trevino. And big is a bloody nuisance sometimes, say I, especially when you're fourteen and the band is playing a slow foxtrot and the girl you want to dance with only comes up to your belt.

Anyway. Soon I was heading north again up the San Fernando Valley, putting along comfortably in the inside lane with the Sunday drivers and old maids. On the radio, Kenny Rogers was telling me that you gotta know when to hold them and when to fold them. I told Kenny I already knew, but I was lying. I was for some inexplicable reason as bad a poker player as that anecdotal dog who played a steady game but had one major fault – every time he got a decent hand he wagged his tail.

I turned off the freeway where the sign told me to and some ten minutes later found Parson's Crossing right where it was supposed to be, not that there was a lot of it to find. It was one of those towns that are so small the signs that read 'You are now entering' and 'You are now leaving' were both on the same post. There was a crossroads and a general store with a gas pump out front selling a kind of gas you've never heard of and a dinette beside it and a house or two and a scrapyard and a combination Farmer's Insurance and John Deere agency with a horse in a small paddock out back. There was also a low, cinderblock building with an American flag flying from a mast out front. I deduced without too much brain work that must be the place so I pulled in and parked beside a dusty Jeep Wagoneer that was painted in the official state colors of green and white.

When I got out of my foolish car and stretched, it was so quiet I could hear the horse next door laughing to itself. I went up the two wide steps and in through the front door and explained my needs to a uniformed gent who was holding down the front desk and doubling as the switchboard operator.

'You'll be wanting Ricky,' he said, glancing up at an old-fashioned wall clock. 'He's usually back by four.' It was then right on three thirty. 'You're welcome to park yourself on that bench over there or you could take yourself over to Mae's for a piece of her famous pecan pie.'

'Mae's famous homemade pecan pie, eh?' I said, smacking my lips. 'Sounds mighty tasty.'

'Well, it ain't,' the man said. 'It ain't homemade, neither. And her coffee's terrible, too. I oughta know, I'm married to her.'

He was right, her coffee was terrible, I could hardly finish the second cup. I was paying the bill when another Wagoneer went by the dinette and turned in at the flag. I strolled back over and said to the gent at the desk, 'Was that Ricky?'

'Looked like him to me,' he said, pointing behind him. 'Second on your left.' I went down the hall, passed one office and knocked on the door of the second. A typed card informed me that it was the office of Ranger Enrique Castillo.

'It's not locked,' said a voice from within. I figured that meant I was to enter, so I did. Ricky was sitting at an aluminum desk making notes in pencil on a large map.

'Hi. Be right with you,' he said, so I sat in the metal chair facing him and folded my hands politely on my lap. Ricky was a dark-haired, dark-skinned Latin with a thin, handsome face and tired brown eyes. Young thirties. Zapata mustache. He was wearing a light green shirt, dark green jodhpurs and boots. A forest ranger's parka and cap were on a coatrack behind him. The walls were bare except for several drawings of birds done in colored pencil.

After a minute he expertly folded up the map without having to refold any of it, a skill I have never been able to master, and put it away in a cardboard file that the map had been covering. Then he put the file away in a green cabinet, then he smiled at me and offered me a Camel.

When I declined, he lit up with a box match. After blowing the match out he waited for a minute, felt the tip to see that it had cooled, then put the match back in the box the other way round.

'And what can I do for you, sir?' he then asked me.

I took out my investigator's license and passed it over. He looked at it curiously.

'Never seen one of these before, Mr Daniel,' he said. He turned it over to examine the back, which was blank, then he handed it across to me again.

Another ranger, a young, good-looking fellow, wearing the same sort of uniform as Ricky, poked his head in the door. He had a carton under one arm.

'Sorry, amigo,' he said. 'Didn't know you were busy.'

'Nada,' said Ricky. 'Mr Daniel, Ranger Thomas L.L. DeMarco, known to all as Tommy.'

'A pleasure, sir,' said Ranger DeMarco, giving me a nice smile. 'Hey, amigo, look at what I got from the folks, I got your hothouse corn, I got your fresh garden tomatoes, I got your avocados, and I got your fresh smoked ham. All for you. I already kept more than I can use.'

'Hey, amigo,' said Ricky. 'Many thanks from the whole Castillo clan.' Tommy waved and disappeared.

'So where do all those goodies come from?' I asked.

'His folks have got a farm up north,' Ricky said. 'Outside Modesto somewhere, and his mother worries he's not eating properly. Now. What brought you out here to these tranquil parts, Mr Daniel?' he asked.

'Corderos, Señor Castillo,' I said in my high-school Spanish. Actually, 'cordero' is the word for lamb, not sheep, but I didn't know the word for sheep. Señor Castillo's tired brown eyes went suddenly untired, then wary, then blank.

'Lambs? What lambs? Are you sure you've come to the right department, Mr Daniel?'

Well I wasn't positive but I was sure surer than I'd been a few minutes ago.

'I believe so,' I told him, 'if you can confirm that you are the person in charge of that tract of state forestry land that runs up against Wonderland Park.'

'I am one of them,' he said carefully. 'Tommy's the other.'

'How large an area is it?'

He shrugged. 'Medium. About twenty thousand acres.'

I nodded as if I knew how big an acre was. Well, who does?

'May I ask how familiar you are with the area, or at least your part of it?'

'Very,' he said shortly, 'if you're talking about the southern half – the part nearest Wonderland Park. I wouldn't say I knew every tree but I damn near do. Now it's your turn.'

I couldn't see any reason not to tell Ricky everything, so I did. I told him of my call from Olivia, the visit to Wonderland Park, and that I had come to the conclusion after examining the scene of the crimes that someone had gone in from outside, probably over the outer fence, probably at night and probably on foot. The service road that circled the park connected with the main road into the park inside the main entrance, which was firmly locked at night. And, according to Olivia, you could rule out anybody trying to get away with five sheep during the day. So, I told Señor Castillo, who was looking more and more worried for some reason, that it seemed the only place the thief could have gone with the corderos was into forestry land, like I said, on foot.

He thought for a minute, then he said, 'Would it not have been possible for someone to have parked a car or truck outside the front gate and to have left that way?'

'Remotely possible,' I said, watching him go through his match routine again after lighting up another cigarette. 'But how would he get the corderos to the car or truck? He'd have to lug them one at a time either through the park or around the service road, then chuck them over the front gate somehow. Doesn't sound likely to me. Then, of course, there's the question, why? Who knows, maybe the bears out there got 'em but I always thought bears, except for those white ones, were vegetarians. Nuts. Wild onions. Honey.'

'You thought correctly,' Ricky said. 'At least as far as the bears go. Anything else?'

'Not a lot,' I said. 'You tell me you know the area just north of the park very well. OK. I think someone's hiding out there. I think he pops in to the park once in a while and helps himself to selected items from something called Ye Cat 'n' Fiddle and who knows where else. Maybe he gets tired of squirrel stew. Maybe he likes to talk to the animals. Why he's started stealing corderos, God knows. Maybe he's been there so long sheep are starting to look good to him. Maybe he's an Australian sheep herder who's lonely. Maybe he wants to be caught, doing something as obvious as that.'

'Say that again?' Ricky made a grimace of pain.

'Maybe he wants to be caught. You know, like a cry for help.'

'Oh, shit,' said Señor Castillo. 'Shit, shit, shit.' He got up and looked out the window. What the hell, I looked out of it too. I don't know what he saw but from where I was sitting all I could make out were some trees, some fields, and some low hills in the distance. And the odd strato-cumulus or two.

'Oh, shit,' he said again. 'It's probably Chico.'

'Who's Chico?' I asked him.

'My wife's kid brother,' he said.

CHAPTER FOUR

It was later that noche.

I was sitting in the Castillos' kitchen eating seconds of some Nicaraguan specialty that Ricky's wife Ellena had piled on my plate over my weak objections. It was dark, meaty, and sizzling hot, like me on a good day. The Castillos' six-year-old daughter Margarita had just been taken off to bed after giving me a loud, wet, beso – kiss to you non-linguists. When Ellena came back she squeezed a half a lime over some shredded lettuce and avocado and watched me sternly until I took a bite. She was a tiny woman, extremely pretty, pregnant again. Like all the black Nicaraguans, she came from the sparsely populated Atlantic coast region, I had been informed during the first course, a rice and vegetable soup. With the repast Ricky and I drank San Miguel beer, Ellena a bottled water I had never heard of. I had fairly strong thoughts about bottled water, in fact I still do, but I kept them to myself.

The Castillos lived in a compact, self-contained bungalow in a row of roughly similar dwellings on Parkside, in Inglewood, close enough to LAX to be aware of the almost continuous air traffic overhead but fortunately not so close that plates rattled every time a 747 took off or landed. The kitchen was small and spotless, the wee yard around the house obviously tended with great affection. A large sign on the gate of the Castillos' driveway warned the unwary to beware, there was a large, unchained dog on the premises, but I hadn't seen any sign of one. Too bad, I like dogs, even large, unchained ones.

Well. The Castillos' story was briefly thus and so: during those desperate times a few years back in Nicaragua when the Somocistas burnt, tortured and slaughtered, to say nothing of looted everything lootable, one's choices were few but clearly defined, as they tend to be in all countries ruled by power-crazed madmen – one stayed and shut up, one stayed and fought, one stayed and collaborated or one got the hell out. These choices only applied to those still living, of course. Ellena's brother, Tomás, known affectionately as Chico – roughly translated, Tiny – took to the hills and joined one of the guerrilla bands that were later to unite and be known as Sandinistas. Ricky, Ellena and their daughter got out by boat up the Atlantic, or more accurately, the Caribbean, coast, embarking at Puerto Cabezas. They got off at Vigía Chico and then made their way, mostly by bus, up through Mexico. The daughter was two at the time. They crossed into the United States legally at Nuevo Laredo with one suitcase, a pot or two, and a few crumpled Nicaraguan cordobas worth about ten dollars US.

But the Castillos managed, if not to prosper, at least to more than survive. Ricky had a trade and excellent English as he had worked for an American-owned banana plantation back home. Most important of all, the Castillos had a sponsor, their Uncle Pepe, a well-connected businessman and American citizen who had not only helped them obtain their immigration papers but helped Ricky to prepare for the State of California civil servant's exam, which he easily passed. Ricky liked his work and was good at it, his wife had several Nicaraguan friends and their area of Inglewood, although violent, still retained enough middle-class families to give it some kind of stability.

Chico, three years younger than Ellena, unmarried, a fierce patriot as his father had been, barely survived. After two years in the bush he was taken prisoner by a Guardia patrol near the Honduran border although at the time he was merely planting maize for the old widow who had let him use an empty hammock in her home. Then the Guardia proceeded to fry out Chico's brains, using a primitive hand-operated generator. Although Ricky wouldn't say so in front of his wife, I assumed that the Guardia had only started on his brains after they had finished frying off his balls.

Pues. Time passes, as it does.

Un dia (one fine day) what was left of Chico arrived on the Castillos' doorstep, thanks once more to the intervention of Tío Pepe and some of his mysterious business contacts. But Chico presented a considerable problem for the Castillos. Although most of the time he was docile and childlike he had occasional flashes of viciousness. Also, he wouldn't or couldn't enter any large building and to him the Castillos' small bungalow was a large building. Also, he had no papers. For a week Chico slept in a hammock in the garden then his brother-in-law installed him in a disused toolshed that was well hidden among the trees some two miles north of Wonderland Park in a part of the forest that naturally came under Ricky's area of responsibility. And there he had been, on his own, except for regular visits from his brother-in-law and once a month or so, his sister, for the past two years.

'Maybe he wants to be caught,' Ricky said to his wife. 'When Mr Daniel said that I started to worry for him.'

'Pobre Chico,' she said. 'Pobrecito.' She folded her hands on her tummy protectively and smiled sadly at me. I smiled sadly back at her. Pobre Chico is right. Poor all the chicos (and the grandes, if you don't mind) in all the lost paradises and filthy cities.

'Well, he can't go on stealing sheep is one thing for sure,' I said. 'If it turns out it is him.'

'I think it is,' Ricky said quietly. 'It's happened before.'

'With sheep?'

'No, other animals.'

'What does he do with them?' I asked him. But Ricky wouldn't say, right then, he just shook his head in disapproval or pity or both.

I took my leave a few minutes later after saying no thanks to coffee but many thanks to them and particularly Ellena for the fine meal. We had agreed that all three of us should pay Chico a visit as soon as possible and had set it up for the following afternoon after Ricky got off work.

On the way back to the Valley I passed Hollywood Boulevard. On a whim, or more accurately on a sudden thirst, I turned south on it and stopped at the first bar I came to. It was called the Stagecoach. I wondered if it would take me somewhere I wanted to go but then, after standing on the corner there at Cherokee and Hollywood for a moment or two taking in the scene, I decided I'd settle for anywhere but where I was. Maybe it was pobre Chico's story, maybe it was the time of the month or the year of my life but it felt like one of those nights that held no promise, only memories and trouble. The fabled Hollywood Boulevard was as dirty as a Dead End Kid's face, gray as a wino's undershirt. And in the Stagecoach, no saxophones wailed in the background, no sad frail in silver lamé sat on the corner stool toying idly with a cocktail stirrer waiting for she knew not what. A black hooker in gold mini shorts sat on the corner stool, waiting for what she knew all too well.

I had a brandy and ginger ale, then another one. The hooker made a great deal out of the simple chore of putting a quarter in the jukebox. I had another brandy and ginger. The hooker finally scored, and left with her client by the side door. I wondered if there wasn't somewhere some small town where the trains still stopped, where a smiling porter would help me down and direct me to Miss Lilly's, where only single gents stayed, where kids played on the Civil War cannon and the Town Hall clock was frozen at a quarter to four. Maybe there'd even be a sign in the window of the hardware store – 'Willing Boy Wanted'.

What the hell. I don't get depressed often, but, 'Slice me and do I not bleed too?' someone once said. I think it was Yogi Berra.

I moved on to Dave's Corner Bar over the hill and down in the Valley, like me, bandied a few words of wisdom with Bill over a couple of games of pool, had a quick one at the Two-Two-Two, then a couple of slow ones at the Three Jacks, then a nightcap at the Cloverleaf. Then I ran out of thirst so I went home, looked in on Mom, saw she was safely tucked up in bed, drank three glasses of water, then, more or less safely, tucked myself up in my little trundle bed.

The following morning, 11 January, I broke the last of my New Year's resolutions – I swore at my mother, that dear little sweet gray-haired mother o'mine. I'm no purveyor of cheap gossip, no tell-tale, there's not one ounce of the catty in me but if there's one thing I hate it's when she eats melba toast at the breakfast table when I've got a hangover.

When I arrived at the office I saw that for once the mail had got there first, so I popped into the Taco-Burger next door but two where Mrs Morales sold me a large coffee to go. As I've just mentioned, there's not a hint of the bitchy in me but was not the gorgeous Señora Morales carrying a touch more avoirdupois around the hips these days?

Back at the office, I unlocked the massive Bowman & Larens safe that took up most of the washroom, then took out and set up both the computer and my electric typewriter just in case, then I attacked the morning post. Into the wastebasket went something beginning 'This will introduce you to the Studio City Jewish Over-Forties Singles' Club'. Following it went yet another unwanted offer from the *Reader's Digest*, this time for a series of imitation hand-tooled leather volumes depicting the history of the Old West. I reckoned I was already having enough problems with the New West. Out went 'America's Foremost painter of cats is proud to present for the first time a limited edition . . .' An ex-girlfriend of mine, Mae Schroeder, now Mrs Lionel B. Jefferies, had thoughtfully taken the time during her honeymoon in Mazatlán to send me a postcard of three pelicans winging their way into the Pacific sunset. I'd seen a lot of Mae the year before, then she'd upped and married a condo salesman. That says something about someone but I'm not quite sure what, or who. Then, oh lucky day, yet another cheery postcard, from a twerp I knew, a punk twerp, a nitwit named Sara who was up in Northern California visiting a friend of her late mother. 'Having wonderful time,' it read, 'Glad you're not here.'

The phone rang, I answered it promptly. It was my landlord, my office landlord, Elroy.

'If it's the rent, I paid already,' I said. 'Stop pestering me or I'll call a cop.'

He laughed. He laughed a lot, Elroy. Of course he was very rich and usually very stoned, which makes it easier.

'Got a mo, bro?' he asked. 'Cause if you do, I got a small problem.'

'Well, I got a mo,' I said, shuffling through the last of the mail. No bills, but no new work, either. 'Want me to drop by?'

'OK, but come up the back way, will you?'

'Sure,' I said. 'Be right over.'

I hung up, packed things away, tidied up, locked up and drove the short distance to my landlord's apartment building and when I say it was his, I mean he owned it, plus the development that included my office, plus several other buildings scattered through that part of the Valley known as Studio City. Not quite knowing what was up, I parked down the street a bit from his building, went into the alley alongside, through the service door and up six flights of the firestairs to his penthouse apartment. His doorbell cunningly played the first few notes of that Beatles number, 'Yesterday'.

Elroy let me in. He was a man in his early twenties, with an almost perfectly square, tanned, unlined face, his shoulder-length blond hair held neatly at the back by a small leather napkin-ring affair. He was usually to be found wearing shades, antique jeans, worn T-shirts and twenty-nine-cent flip-flops, but that morning he was in a dark two-piece suit, button-down shirt, tie and proper shoes.

He led me into the front room, opened the french doors leading out to the balcony, then went outside and peeked cautiously over the low balcony wall. He gestured for me to join him, so I did. He pointed downwards. I looked downwards, through the retractable glass roof of the building's swimming pool.

'See that?' he whispered.

'Yes,' I whispered back. 'It looks just like a girl with nothing covering her top.'

'It is,' he said. 'Come on.'

We moved back into the sitting room and made ourselves comfortable, me on a canvas-covered sofa, he on a canvas director's chair.

'That's not only a girl,' he said, 'that's a tenant, 2-B. Gloria Linnear. Gorgeous Gloria.'

'So what's up with her?'

Elroy sighed. 'Gorgeous Gloria is on the game,' he said. 'I wouldn't mind the occasional customer but she's turning so many tricks in her pad I'm thinking about putting in a check-in counter. Gorgeous Gloria must go.' He took a little silver hash pipe out of a pocket, lit up, took a hit and offered it to me. I declined.

'Well, you're the landlord,' I said. 'Why don't you just chuck her out?'

He sighed again, then smiled at me, or was it leered.

'Because she's been up here,' he said. 'Often.'

I raised my eyebrows as high as they would go.

'You dog,' I said.

'It's one of the trials of being a young, good-looking, rich landlord,' he said. 'It's not all fun, you know.'

I said I didn't know and didn't want to.

'Anyway, it was, needless to say, before I copped she was doing business, we got stoned a few times, had a laugh or two, a tear or two. So if I give her the axe, what do you think the first thing is she's going to do to me?'

'Tell the Narcs you're a dangerous dope addict, like you are,' I said.

'And that hassle I do not need,' he said. 'I already got done once for it a few years ago. So it can't come from me, the bad news. And I don't want to call the cops on her even if I could, what do I care what she does with her free time, am I a member of the Moral Majority all of a sudden? But I'm starting to get flak from all of her neighbors.'

'So you thought you'd get old Vic to do the dirty work for you, eh?' I said. 'Typical. When would you like her out?'

'End of the month?'

'No problem,' I said. 'I'll think of something. When does she usually start work, if I may put it like that?'

'After her swim,' he said. 'Like early afternoon.'

'OK,' I said. 'I'll pop back to the office, pick up a few things, then come back and have a word with her.'

'Amigo, you're my main man.' He got out of his chair and brushed some invisible lint off one trouser leg. 'Listen, if I haven't been my usual cheery self today it's because I got to go somewhere.'

'I figured,' I said, getting up myself. 'Neat tie. Getting married? Going to church?'

'Wrong,' he said. 'Going to the Forest Hills Funeral Home with my sister.'

'Is it a year already?'

He nodded. One year ago most of his immediate family including his father and mother had been killed when a drunk doing well over a hundred miles an hour skipped the central divider on the San Diego Freeway and collided head on with his family's car. Six dead in all.

'Goddamn it,' I said. 'Well, don't forget to comb your hair first, it looks awful.' It didn't really but what else are you going to say?

I left the way I came. I didn't see anyone on the way down. During the drive back to my office I had a little think about Gloria which led to a thought or two about another girl I'd once known pretty well who also made her living looking at ceilings, she was one of those rare Polish beauties that mining towns like Gary occasionally produce. She was dead now. A lot of people were dead now, but few died the way she did. I didn't have anything to do with her getting killed but I didn't have anything to do with her getting unkilled, either. It is apparent even to me that you can't rewrite history but you can't help wondering once in a while what would have happened if you had been smarter or quicker or tougher. Or somebody else. What the hell.

I picked up the necessary at my office, then wasted a little time at a nearby hamburger stand, Fran's over on Del Monte, where they knew me well, leisurely disposing of three hotdogs, mustard and relish only, and a root beer, then I did a chore or two, so it was coming up to two o'clock by the time I got back to Elroy's. Again, I parked down the street a way as my Technicolor Nash wasn't exactly the type of vehicle a man in the profession I was about to adopt would be seen dead in.

I went in the front this time, past the 'No Vacancy' sign, then out past the pool and up one flight to 2-B. When there was no answer to my polite knock, I tried again not so politely. Still no answer. I leaned my battered face against the door and said loudly, 'Miss Linnear, we know you're in there. Open up, please.'

I heard some noises from inside, then the sound of a bolt lock being drawn back, then the door opened the few inches the chain lock would let it.

'Miss Linnear. Good to see you. Moriarty, Vice.' I flashed her my badge and ID.

'Can I see your ID again, please?'

'Certainly.' I showed it to her again. It looked real enough

29

because it was real, I'd wheedled it out of my brother one time, likewise the badge. When she was done looking at the ID she opened the door properly and took a look at me. I took a look at her right back and figured I easily got the best of the deal. What she saw was someone who was tall and, in the dark, handsome, as that idiot twerp Sara once put it, about the size of Conan the Barbarian but with slightly less muscle tone. And with a face out of a spare-parts catalogue. What I saw was a striking young girl who looked no more than twenty or so, with short, curly blond hair still a little damp, regular features and a beautiful mouth with just a touch of pink lipstick on it. She was wrapped in a man's bathrobe that was so long it almost hid her bare tootsies. Her toenails were pink, too. Gorgeous Gloria was right.

'And what do you want?'

'Just a quick word,' I said. 'It won't take but a moment. We can do it out here in the hall if you want, I don't mind.' I gave her a friendly grin. A friend of mine once said my friendly grins are about as friendly as a one-armed Scotsman in a boarding house at mealtime but he was in real estate and you know how those fellows exaggerate.

'Well, I mind,' she said. 'Come in if you're coming.' I went in. It was just another apartment, but with potted plants hanging everywhere. In one corner was a stuffed giraffe, it must have been as tall as I was.

'Now what,' she said, 'the third degree?'

I opened up my windbreaker to get a notebook from the inside pocket and also to give her a peek at the Police Positive in the shoulder holster. I flipped the notebook open, not letting her see the pages were blank. Then I rattled off in a matter-of-fact monotone.

'Seventh January 4.25. Male caucasian, forties, car license number 835 B C C. Same date, 5.30, caucasian, 85 Chevy . . .' and so on and so on. I did this at some speed so she wouldn't have time to really think about it as I was of course making it all up. Then I glanced over at the closed door leading to the bathroom and gave her a wink.

She shook her adorable head.

'The boys in blue,' she said, 'will get you every time. So what do you want from me? A free sample?' She licked her top lip. 'It would give you something to remember when you're old and gray.' She came closer to me and slipped her belt off. She came still closer. She was a little thing. She had lovely tanned little breasts. She smelt delicious.

'I'm old and gray already, sweetheart,' I said, putting a little distance between us. 'Do yourself up, you'll get goose-bumps and so will I.'

'Gay power lives again,' she said scornfully. She took a pack of cigarettes out of her pocket and lit up with a gold Ronson. She blew the smoke in my direction. 'So what's your plan, officer? You going to arrest bad old me?' She batted her eyelashes at me.

'Nope,' I said. 'All I want is for you to find somewhere else to live. You've got til the end of the month.'

She looked surprised. 'That's it?'

'That's it, there ain't no more,' I said.

'Well, scoobie-doo,' she said. 'All in all, I think I'd rather be arrested; I'd be back in time for the six o'clock news.'

'Oh, but think of the hassle,' I said. 'Lawyer, bail bond, another few lines on your sheet. And there's nothing to prevent me from dropping by tomorrow and tomorrow and tomorrow, as what's-his-name once put it.'

'Well, what's-his-name can forget it,' she said.

'And I can forget about whoever's in there,' I said, gesturing to the bedroom, 'if you're a good girl.'

'All right,' she said. 'You don't have to go on and on. I do have a few brains left.'

'Thank you, Miss Linnear,' I said, putting the notebook away and heading for the door. 'It's been a pleasure.'

'Yeah,' she said. 'A million laugh. What I don't get is

what's in it for you.' She looked at me suspiciously. 'Unless you're doing it for the boy wonder upstairs.'

'Never heard of him,' I said. 'And there's nothing in it for me at all. I'm just trying to help my poor brother find a decent apartment in the neighborhood. He's handicapped, you see, polio, and he needs a place to live near where he works.'

She shook her head. 'Ain't love wonderful,' she said.

'Try and leave the place tidy for him, O K?' I said on my way out. 'He'd appreciate that.' She slammed the door behind me.

'Shakespeare, dummy,' she called through the door. 'What's-his-name. Tomorrow and tomorrow.'

'I was sure it was the Beatles,' I called back. 'Live and learn.'

CHAPTER FIVE

I strolled to my car feeling all in all not displeased with the way I'd handled my latest little chore. Life is not all big chores, you know, and mine in particular. I usually had three or four jobs, if they could be called that, going on at any one time. Some got resolved fairly quickly, some I gave up on, some were yearly security contracts that only needed my attention every couple of weeks, bits and pieces, you might say. I plan to write a small monograph on the subject of bits and pieces some day as soon as I find out what a monograph is.

The timing being about right, after I left Elroy's I drove over the Hollywood Hills and down to Inglewood where I picked up Ellena and her daughter. The daughter we dropped off at a friend's house a few blocks away, then I got on the northbound freeway just in time to join the afternoon exodus. Ellena had little to say on the journey, worried as she was about pobre Chico.

When we got to Parson's Crossing, Ricky and his buddy Tommy were sitting out on the edge of the side porch, swinging their heels and putting away after-work beers. As I was parking, Ricky said something to his friend, crumpled up his empty tin, tossed it into a wire bin and came over to join us. He helped his wife out of the car, kissed her cheek, asked her how she was. She smiled up at him and said she was fine. We all got in the front seat of Ricky's Jeep and took off. Tommy watched us go.

'How far is it?' I asked Ricky.

'Twenty minutes' drive, maybe a ten-minute walk,' he said. 'You sure you're all right, Mama? You know how bouncy it gets, would you be happier waiting for us? You could wait at Mae's.'

'If you do,' I said, 'stay away from her pecan pie.'

Ellena shook her head stubbornly. 'I come,' she said. She patted her husband's arm reassuringly.

He shrugged. 'What can you do?'

'What did you tell Tommy?' I asked him.

'Nothing.'

'You must have told him something. How often does Ellena show up here after work with a tall, handsome gringo?'

'Oh. I said we were going to look at a piece of property over near Walton that me and my uncle might buy. OK?'

'OK. Have you ever mentioned anything at all to him or anybody else about Chico?'

'Never. Why?'

'Just asking,' I said.

We drove in silence for a while. Ellena laid her head against her husband's shoulder. She took it away when we turned off the paved road on to a dirt one. About fifty yards farther on was a locked gate that was well signposted with warnings of no admittance to the public, and why. Ricky handed me a key, I jumped out, undid the padlock, waited until the Jeep was through the gate, locked up again then hopped back in. What a team.

The road got rapidly worse. In some places it had been resurfaced with tree trunks from deadfalls laid side by side and roughly packed with dirt in the gaps. I asked Ricky if there was a lot of that type of road in the reserve.

'Every few miles,' he said, switching into four-wheel drive to take a slippery hill. 'Like a grid. For service access, for in case of fire, for fire breaks, for boundaries so we can identify any section by its coordinates. Up north where Tommy works it gets hillier so the grid isn't as regular.'

'Who put the roads in?'

'The original loggers,' he said. 'All of this is second or

third growth. It's coming on, though. If it had a little more natural water like it does farther north in California it would do even better.'

We pulled up at the top of the rise; Ricky switched off the motor.

'Pretty, eh, querida?' he said in the sudden quiet.

Ellena agreed that it was pretty. I suppose it was, if you think trees are pretty, for that was about it as far as the eye could see, low tree-covered hills rising in the distance to higher tree-covered hills. Me, I reserve the word 'pretty' for things that really are, like Maidenform bras and neon signs of cocktail glasses winking on and off.

'Where's Wonderland Park from here?' I asked Enrique as we were all getting out and stretching.

'You can't see it but it's only about a mile and a half that way,' he said, pointing.

'That way would be south?'

'It would.' He unlocked the trunk, took out a heavy belt that had clipped to it a machete in a leather case, a holster, a canteen which he shook to see that it was full, and one or two other useful objects, then buckled it on. Then he took his wife's hand and we set off into the jungle. Well, forest, if you want to nit-pick, but it was jungle to me. Ellena carried a shopping bag she had brought along.

'What's all the equipment for?' I asked Ricky with exaggerated concern. 'Bears? Wolves? Big Foot?'

'Common sense,' he said. 'If I fell and broke my leg, with the machete I could make a splint and with the gun I could make a noise.'

'And with the canteen you could drink,' I said. 'I get it.'

The going was easy, although I couldn't see any discernible path we were following. The ground underfoot was springy with fallen needles and the trees were far enough apart so we didn't have to hack our way through it with the machete.

'Are there any animals at all here?' I asked Ricky after a bit. 'Just out of curiosity.'

'Plenty,' he said proudly. 'Squirrels, snakes, coyotes, porcupines, shrews, there might be a bobcat or two, coons, I've never seen a wolf but Tommy said he did although it could have been a dog. Maybe someday we'll get bear back, wouldn't that be great?'

'Marvelous,' I said, sneaking a look back over one shoulder. 'Can't wait.'

Quiet. It was quiet in the woods . . . too quiet. What happened to the drums, Carruthers? After another bit Ricky suddenly stopped and pointed up at something. I looked, fearing the worst. Ricky made a bird noise, and darned if the bird didn't answer him.

'Woodpecker,' he whispered.

'Why isn't it pecking?' I whispered back. Ellena giggled.

'It's made its home already,' she said.

'Of course,' I said.

As Ricky had mentioned earlier, it was only about a ten-minute walk. When I was giving a wide berth to something I thought just might be a highly dangerous coral snake but which turned out to be a partly peeled twig, he told me to wait where I was for a moment and went on ahead with his wife. A minute later I heard her call out, 'Chico? It's me. And Rico.' Ricky reappeared almost immediately and beckoned me forward. After a few steps I could see Chico's abode through the trees – a small lean-to maybe ten foot square made out of unpainted weathered logs that had been roughly trimmed, with a tarpaper roof. It had no windows that I could see, but the door was ajar. On the roof was a sort of square wooden box that I supposed acted as the top of a chimney. A rain barrel made from an empty oil drum sat under one of the eaves. Some washing was drying on a cord stretched between two nearby trees. Several animal skins were tacked up on the front wall of the cabin. I could see Ellena down on her knees in the doorway, talking as if to a child she didn't want to frighten.

When I caught up to Ricky I asked him how he had ever found the place, hidden as it was.

'I saw it by accident through the fire-watcher's telescope,' he said. 'You can't see it from here now because of the new growth but there's a fire tower way over there somewhere. I go up there maybe once a month to look over my empire and win a little money playing gin. I took Chico up there once.'

Ellena got up, brushed the knees of her slacks, and came over to join us. She seemed upset.

'How is he?' Ricky asked her.

'Malo,' she said, shaking her head. 'He'll hardly even talk to me. I told him you brought a friend who had to see him, it was serious, but I don't know . . .'

'Let's go, amigo,' said Ricky. I followed him the few steps to the shed, then we stepped inside, me having to duck considerably. Inside it was dark and slightly chilly. In one corner a fireplace had been built out of natural stone. And, as I'd supposed, the wooden box on the roof was the top of a cleverly designed, homemade wooden chimney. It had obviously been constructed with some considerable skill, as had the wooden table and chair, bedframe and a couple of three-legged stools. There was a Coleman lamp on the table, a stack of firewood beside the fireplace. A large tin box. Several smaller tin boxes. On top of the bedframe was a thin slab of foam and a neatly folded duvet. A row of pots hung from nails by the fire, another one hung by a chain over the ashes. A machete and a whetstone on a shelf. A couple of wooden candle holders. Bunches of dried herbs were strung up on the wall beside the fire, also a string of dried mushrooms and one of dried peppers. One wall had been reserved for Chico's art collection—there were several drawings of birds he had done, I found out, similar to the ones in Ricky's office, some colored photographs of his homeland, and a small Nicaraguan flag – blue and white horizontal stripes.

Pobre Chico was sitting hunched on one of the stools in front of the dead fire. He looked to be no taller than his tiny sister. He had long, dark hair, unshaven face, eyes white in the gloom, dressed in clean jeans and a much-darned sweater. Plaited headband to hold back his hair. Sneakers. No socks. I wondered briefly how he kept as clean as he did.

I didn't understand all that was said during the next half hour or so but I picked up some of it and Ricky or Ellena translated some of it then and some of it later, so I'll describe the events in the order they happened to keep it simple.

First, after a moment Ellena squatted down – with some difficulty, because of her condition – beside the fireplace and began to rake out the ashes. Chico gently pushed her away and took over the chore himself, which was the first sign of life from him, no doubt his sister's intention, as she flashed us a satisfied look as she went and sat down carefully in the one chair. Chico opened up one of the tin boxes, took out dry kindling and some pine cones, and soon had a fire going right under the hanging pot. This he took down, rinsed out, refilled with fresh water from a clay jar, and hung it up again to heat. Then out of another box he laid out cups, sugar in a glass jar and some dry leaves in another jar about which I feared the worst. Ricky sat on the bed; I joined him there. Ellena chatted to her brother and before long he was answering her back, albeit in monosyllables. He smiled once when she pointed to her tummy and said, 'Bigger than you already.'

It was obvious we weren't going to get down to the real reason for our visit until the tea ceremony was over so we made small talk until Chico had added some of the leaves to the hot water and then poured us all out a cup. It was as bad as I'd feared, even with three spoons of sugar in it, but we sipped it and made appreciative noises. Chico finished his in one gulp, not a bad idea, then opened up the care package his sister had brought him. Some more sugar, a half a dozen tins of sardines and tuna, fruit, some condensed milk, flour, a tin of Crisco, extra candles. He looked at each item carefully, sometimes reading the labels, then put everything away neatly in the appropriate tin or on the right shelf. Then, in thanks, he kissed his sister on the top of her head and gave his brother-in-law one abrupt handshake. Then Ricky, figuring it was time, began asking him about sheep, and none too gently either. He went over to him, looked down, then pointed at him and said,

'Chico, was it you?'

Chico hung his head.

'Look at me,' Ricky said. Chico looked up. 'Was it you?'

Finally, Chico nodded.

'Why?'

Chico shrugged. He didn't know.

'When?'

He forgot.

'What did you do to them?'

'I killed them.'

'How?'

He held out his two hands; he didn't look strong enough to strangle a marshmallow.

'Then what?'

Chico said he carried them down the path to the gate and threw them over on to the service road.

'Then what?'

'Then I took a swim.'

Ellena and I looked at each other, uncomprehending.

'A swim? Where?'

'With my friend the big fish, I swim there often.'

Jesus wept. He was only jumping in with one of the dolphins in the middle of the night.

Chico smiled at the memory. 'He liked it. He knew when I was coming. He'd be waiting.'

'Then what?' Ricky asked him.

'I buried the sheep in the woods. I was ashamed.' Chico hung his head again. Ricky ruffled his hair none too gently.

'Hell,' he said, 'what's a few stupid sheep, right Mr Daniel?'

'Right on,' I said. 'Smelly critters.'

'But understand, Chico, it could be serious trouble if it happens again, for you and me and Ellena. Maybe next time they don't send a friend of ours, like Mr Daniel, to investigate, maybe next time they send the police and maybe the police take you away where you can't have your own house anymore and where we can't visit you. I know you forget after that you do these things, but they have to stop.'

'What can we do?' Ellena asked.

'I don't know,' Ricky said. 'Maybe we can move him to another cabin as far up north as we can get, maybe I'll have to talk to Tommy.'

Chico looked frightened.

'Just as nice,' Ricky assured him, 'same size, with all your things, and we'd still come and see you, but you'd be twenty miles away from the nearest bloody sheep or big fish. But I don't know. What's twenty miles when you get like that?'

Ricky looked at me for help. I didn't have a lot, in fact I wasn't sure I had any, in fact I didn't know what the hell to do for pobre Chico. I couldn't see him being any better off in a hospital, even if what he was suffering from was curable, which I doubted. To move him farther back into the woods might keep him out of trouble for a while but I couldn't help thinking that his recent actions really were a cry for help after all. But I'm no shrink, as you may have suspected by now, so what did I know? But maybe a real shrink could come up with something helpful, that was a thought. Then I had another one. I asked Ricky to ask Chico if he had lifted the occasional hamburger patty from Ye Cat 'n' Fiddle on his midnight prowls.

'Hamburger, no,' Chico told him. 'Chocolate, si.'

Which reminded me. I took out the six-pack of Mars Bars Ellena had suggested I bring along for Chico and passed it over. He inspected it carefully, gave me the same sort of one-pump handshake he had given his brother-in-law, then stowed the candy away carefully in one of his tin boxes.

We left shortly afterwards. Ellena gave her kid brother a hug. Ricky told him to be good, he'd see him in a few days. I said, 'Adios, Chico, suerte,' which means, lotsa luck, pal. As we were about to disappear into the wilderness, Chico came running after us with one of his bird sketches in one hand. He gave it to me, shook my hand again, then ran back towards his cabin. I've still got it, in my bedroom, as a matter of fact. It shows a large blue bird with its beak inside the beak of a small blue bird. What exactly they think they are doing I do not know.

No one said very much on the way back, either in the jungle or during the drive south. Ricky did tell me, when asked, that Chico had killed animals before, once a neighbor's dog when he was living with the Castillos, which was one of the reasons they had moved him. He said Chico seemed to go crazy about once every six months, but the incidents weren't getting any more frequent. However, the incident with the sheep was the first time he had ever killed more than one animal, so maybe it was building up. Did I know Chico was a eunuch? I said the thought had crossed my mind. Then he asked me what I thought we should do.

'God knows,' I said. 'I have a doctor friend who might take a look at him as a favor but he won't be back til the end of the week. According to you he should be OK until then. If he thinks something can be done medically, well, I hear papers can be arranged if you know the right people, maybe even some kind of army discharge documents so he could get treated for free in a Vets' hospital. Something that should be done for sure is for you to pay for the cost of replacing those corderos, and pronto, so the sheep lady can sleep nights; it won't be much because the lady can get them cheap from a guy we know. Then we can take our time and see what else we can come up with.'

'Pobre Chico,' said Ellena. She began to cry quietly, the tears running steadily down her thin face.

I took her hand. It was half the size of mine, but a lot prettier.

CHAPTER SIX

When I got home that evening Mom was asleep on the sofa. She'd made a mess trying to cook me some spaghetti sauce, which I cleaned up, then I dropped her off downstairs where she was going to eat with Feeb – a potato chip, mince meat and macaroni casserole, I was informed – then the girls were going to watch sports on ESPN.

I had a date with Evonne, who was the assistant to the vice-principal of St Stephen's, a high school not far from my office. We'd met about six months earlier when I was endeavoring, with considerable success, it turned out, to rid the school of some of its more undesirable elements, such as sixteen-year-old pushers and a head of security who was on the take. We had been seeing each other a couple of times a week since then. Evonne was blond, blue-eyed and cute as Blondie Bumstead as played by Penny Singleton, remember her? Like that. Aside from her legs, there was another item I liked about Evonne – she never wanted to have a serious talk with me in bed at two thirty in the morning. I'd never managed to be in bed with her at two thirty in the morning, but still. Don't get me wrong, she had her faults, serious ones – she was indifferent to dogs, she liked all kinds of marrows and squashes, she was hopeless with makeup and was easily the world's most irritating driver. However, what am I if not tolerant?

We had a theater date, thank you, that evening, so I dressed with extra care – subdued (comparatively) Hawaiian shirt, sand-colored suede jacket, tan cords, moccasins. A dash of Brut. Clean undies. Wow.

I picked her up at her place just after eight; she had the

back half of a ranch-style house down on Beeker's Canyon that came with a good-sized garden thrown in where she actually grew marrows and summer squashes and assorted other greenery. My sweet was attired in a pair of skin-tight black toreadors, silver high heels, a scoop-neckline blouse and over all her old high-school letter sweater. Two blue barrettes in her curly blond hair. Lipstick already smudged. I smudged it some more in the car when we stopped at the first red light. It was cherry flavored, my second favorite.

We were headed toward her school to see something called *Waiting for Godot*. Evonne told me that the author, whose name I forget if ever I knew it, had an eightieth birthday coming up so the school drama department was doing three of his plays.

We got there on time, found our seats, said hello to a lot of folks, or at least she did, then the house lights dimmed and the play began. There were these two tramps, see, waiting for someone: one had a sore foot and the other didn't. And that was it. By the end of the interminable first act I'd figured out that the guy they were waiting for was going to be a no-show so I sat out the second half in my car listening to a C & W station on the radio. Now, Dolly Parton, if she had a sore foot I bet she wouldn't sit around complaining all the time. Evonne claimed she wasn't miffed at me for leaving her in the lurch but I noticed she ordered the second most expensive item on the menu at Mario's afterwards, the veal piccata, and also I couldn't help noticing that she didn't invite me in for a nightcap, let alone a little heavy necking back at her place. Maybe I should have waited for that guy a couple of hours longer.

Mañana came knocking at its usual time – too early. When I left home after breakfast Mom was vacuuming the carpets again.

The office was chilly. I was on my knees turning on the gas

44

heater when there was a timid tap-tap at the door. It was unlocked but I politely went to open it anyway for whoever was there.

A woman was there. Middle-aged, white, all wrapped up in a overcoat more suited to back East than California. She had one arm in a new-looking cast and sported a classic shiner.

I asked her to please come in and got her seated in the spare chair across the desk from me. She gave her name as Mrs Mavis Gillespie. I didn't believe her but I let it slide. The Mrs part I believed as she was wearing a plain gold wedding ring.

'What's it about, Mrs Gillespie?' I asked her when she had more or less stopped squirming about in the chair. She raised one hand to her swollen cheek, which I suppose was some sort of answer, then turned away to look out the front window. I didn't bother looking. I knew what was out there. Unless Mr H. Houdini had miraculously come by since I last looked out some three minutes earlier and changed everything into a glittering wonderland complete with capering pixies, what was out there was a small parking lot, then some of those weird Californian palm trees of which all you can see is scabrous trunk because the tops disappear some forty feet up into that yellow murk known as LA air. Oh yes, you could also see a street, Victory, and several million cars.

Finally I said, 'Look, would you like a cup of coffee or something?'

She shook her head.

'Is it your husband?'

This time she nodded slightly. Then, still without looking at me, she said, with a hint of a brogue, 'Please, can you tell me what you charge?'

'Sure,' I said. 'Twenty-five dollars an hour, usually.'

'Why?'

I didn't know what she was getting at, so I said, 'Why not?'

'Why that much?'

I didn't have a clue. 'I find out what psychiatrists are charging these days and half it,' I said.

She nodded, as if that made sense. Maybe it did. From her handbag she took out five five-dollar bills, one at a time, and passed them to me. I got a glimpse of what looked like prayer beads as she did so.

'Thank you, Mrs Gillespie,' I said. 'Would you like a receipt?'

She shook her head again. I was afraid she was going to start staring out the wndow again, so I said, 'Listen, Mrs Gillespie, I know it's difficult to talk about your personal life in front of a stranger, but like a doctor or a lawyer or a priest, I am under oath as well to keep what I hear to myself.' I wasn't really, but so what? 'Also, if I may say so, I've been involved many times before with serious domestic problems.' I hadn't really as no one in my line of work likes to have anything to do with serious domestic problems except for a little harmless divorce work as someone usually got hurt and that someone was usually your well-meaning busybody. I can't honestly say I've got the scars to prove the above statement but I can and will say I've got one scar to prove it and that one a beauty; it was made by boiling water.

Nothing from Mrs Gillespie except that this time she looked around the office instead of out the reinforced plate-glass window. It didn't take her long. My office was about twelve feet by twelve feet, was painted off-white, had a tundra (dark green, dear) carpet and two items on the wall – a fire extinguisher and a calendar of Armenian beauties compliments of my pal Mr Amoyan. Oh yes, there was also a shelf of more or less technical books.

'I can't,' she said suddenly. She started to get to her feet. Her coat fell open slightly; I saw she was wearing a religious medal of some kind on a chain around her neck. I made one more try.

'If it is your husband the choices are pretty clear – stay or go. The police don't like to and indeed can't get involved unless there are repeated assaults and the assaulted party is willing to formally charge her assailant, because unless there is a major change in the situation, such as a jail sentence, the same actions tend to recur, the wife gets blamed and beaten up again. I'm not saying it's easy to leave, there can be a lot of strong reasons against it, children, religion, lack of money, nowhere to go, but at least leaving solves one problem – you can't get beaten up from a distance.'

I think she was listening but I wasn't sure, she still wouldn't volunteer anything. I tried yet again.

'If you're a Catholic I assume you've already had a talk with your priest which didn't help and a talk with your husband which didn't help and I also assume you've tried everything else you can think of before coming here because for a woman like you a man like me must be more or less a last resort. Did you have any idea of the sort of help you might get from me?'

This time she got all the way up, buttoned her coat, and began to walk out. I caught her at the door, I didn't want her money.

'Here,' I said, holding it out. 'On the house.'

I thought she was going to take it but she slapped it out of my hand, hard, and left. I watched her cross the street to the bus stop on the other side and sit down on the bench there, the one that advertised a local kosher funeral home. A Catholic funeral home was what she was going to need, I remember thinking, if she didn't put some mileage between her and her charming husband soon.

I don't know. Sometimes I think I do but sometimes I know I don't. When in doubt, eat, so I closed up and meandered down to Fred's Deli on Ventura. On the way I noticed that Mrs Gillespie was still on the bench although a bus had just pulled out. At Fred's I had my usual second breakfast of cream cheese on onion rolls (two) and a glass of buttermilk. As I was leaving I paused for a chat with Two-to-One Tim, a bookie I knew who lived in Fred's front booth and I put ten bucks down at respectable odds on the Lakers who were playing in Boston that night. Easy money.

Back at the office, I pondered. Then, just to make sure, I called the psychiatrist friend of mine, Art Feldman, who owed me one, the doctor I wanted to have a look at Chico, but as I thought, he was out of town until the end of the week, his answering machine told me. It also told me that in case of emergencies he could be located on the front nine of a golf course somewhere in Southern California. Very funny, Art. But that took care of Chico for the next few days, or rather, didn't. Bits and pieces . . . did I ever expound to you about bits and pieces? In my work there is rarely a beginning, a middle and an end, in real time, like there is in Greek plays, some egghead told me once, where the action moves briskly along in a continuous sequence from onset to startling denouement. Interruptions is what I get, funny messages on answering machines is what I get, Irish ladies who won't talk is what I get. Anyway, if this narrative sometimes seems to be made up of disjointed episodes with brief pauses for eating, drinking, smooching and picking up the drycleaning, it is because it is but a mirror of life. I also read a lot. Paperbacks, but they're books too.

The phone rang. I picked it up. A man wanted to know if I was Victor Daniel. I confessed I was. He wanted to know if I was busy that night. I confessed I wasn't. He said his name was Donald Kalvin and he was a friend of a friend of mine. I asked him which friend. He said Benjamin H. Hanrahan, which meant my pal Benny had been at it again.

'Ah, yes, Benjamin,' I said. 'Good lad. Old friend.' Referring to Benny as a good lad was like referring to Hitler as 'short, careful dresser'. It might be accurate but it was rather missing the point. Benny was a good lad but Benny was a crook was what Benny was, he had his finger in more pies than Little Jack Horner – or was it Tom Thumb? – ever dreamed of, insurance scams being a particular specialty. He'd just bought another half a house in Anaheim which brought him up to five that I knew about and I didn't know everything. One springtime I'd almost married his Aunt Jessica. But there you go.

He was certainly an old friend, though. If I ever thought about it I might find it strange that for someone purportedly in the law-enforcement business like me, so many of my friends were dips, petermen, scam artists, touts, con men and assorted other riff-raff. Perhaps they felt the same way about me. Perhaps the moment someone is your friend you automatically assume a sort of amused tolerance for their little peculiarities. However. Onwards.

'He says you're an expert on private security systems, does that include things like advice on how to set up a neighborhood watch?' Mr Kalvin wanted to know.

'Sure,' I said. 'But the police will do it for free.'

'They'll also take three weeks to get around to us,' Mr Kalvin said. 'And I'm not prepared to wait. Tonight at seven thirty suit you?'

When I said it did, he gave me an address over in festive West Hollywood, and hung up. I did know something about setting up a neighborhood watch but I figured it wouldn't hurt to know a little more so I took the three steps necessary to take me over to my library and actually found something relevant, an old FBI Crime Commission report on violent crimes in the inner cities. It was one of a bunch of stuff my brother had lifted from the LAPD library downtown where he worked and had passed on to me in a desperate attempt to improve my image or education or wage scale or something.

I made some notes; time passed. I typed up the notes. I phoned a sign store down on Santa Monica Boulevard and got some prices from them. I fooled with the computer for a while trying to learn a new program. I visited the Taco-Burger where Mrs Morales' daughter served me something hot, cold, greasy and Mexican. Two bottles of icy Corona eased the pain somewhat.

Then it was the post office to make some copies, then I visited the tool section of the local hardware store, then I picked up the Hollywood Freeway and took it downtown to the old Hall of Justice building on Temple and Broadway. It seemed polite to let the police – or more accurately in this case the Sheriff's Department, as West Hollywood was by contract under its jurisdiction and protection – know what I was up to. The fifteen-story hall, built back in the mid-twenties, is the headquarters of the County Sheriff, an elected official, and his sizable department which polices an area of LA County spread out over three thousand square miles of mountains, sea shore, islands, deserts, suburbs, 7-elevens, porn parlors, corn-dog joints and a great many places where those who thirst for knowledge go – bars. The building itself contains courtrooms and five floors of jail space at the top as well as the head administration offices of the line branches – Patrol, Vice, Burglary, Homicide and Narcotics. The Sheriff's Department has a better reputation than most if not all of the large metropolitan police forces; its recruiting standards are higher (some police forces not even requiring a complete high-school education), the training more severe, especially the physical side of it, the level of commitment and service pride higher as well.

Downtown LA looks like downtown anywhere, it's the only part of Los Angeles that even remotely resembles a normal city. It has tall buildings. It has old hotels. It has rummies and panhandlers, a Chinese section, a Japanese section, a Little Korea, a garment district, the old flower market. I parked half legally, walked to the Hall, stated my business, showed my ID, took the elevator and in no time at all was sitting opposite a guy I knew slightly, a Deputy III name of

Will Mullins who had been one of the Crew in Narcotics until he took a rifle slug in one knee when he stumbled into a holdup in progress when he was off duty one night. Since then he'd been at a desk doing community relations and as I wanted to relate to a community, or part of one, he was the man to see.

He'd put on a little weight, Will, since the last time I'd seen him in a bar down near the Firestone Station in South LA where cops hung out. He'd lost a little hair, too, I was glad to see. And he wore glasses now.

After the usual persiflage that occurs between us he-men types I told him why I was there.

'Professional courtesy, one might call it,' I told him.

'Oh, would one,' he said in a prissy voice. He seemed to be glad to have been interrupted in his paperwork. 'So what would one want from me?'

'You could call up your equivalent in West LA and let him know what I'm up to.'

'I ain't got no equivalent,' he said, 'especially in West LA.' He made a note on a pad. 'So what else?'

'Do you guys provide those neighborhood watch signs?'

'No,' he said, 'but any two-bit printer will.'

'I thought so. I also need a phone number,' I said. 'The local hotline that might get a patrol car without it taking a couple of hours.'

'That I can do,' he said. He flipped through a rotary card file, wrote the number down, and passed it over. 'The man you want there is a Lieutenant Ronald Isaacs, known to all who love him as Abie. What else. What have you been doing? What's life like on the outside? Met any movie stars recently?'

'Nothing but,' I said. 'Why, Tuesday Weld was by my office only yesterday. What about you?'

He grimaced and tossed me over a typewritten sheet of paper that was headed 'The Paradox of Law Enforcement –

The Public's Right Vs. The Policeman's Needs'. Then he handed over another, 'The Contradictions Involved in Forcibly Obtained Evidence'.

'Required reading,' he said. 'These days.'

'Makes a change from *True Detective*,' I said.

'Actually, it's pretty interesting,' he said. 'I'll send you copies if you like. You probably think *Miranda* was some kind of mermaid.'

I thanked him, told him my address was in the book, and got out of there just in time for the rush hour, it was almost three quarters of an hour before I pulled up in front of my apartment. Of course I knew who *Miranda* was, give us a hard one, he played third base with the old Chicago Cubs. Bad field, no hit.

CHAPTER SEVEN

By the time I got to the Kalvins' there were already a couple of dozen people and more were arriving every minute. The house itself was a large, two-story affair on Wilson Crescent, finished in rough white stucco. There were two orange trees in the front yard and something that I guessed was an avocado tree. I found a place to park down the street, locked up, retrieved my genuine leatherette briefcase with the gold initials (not mine) and strolled back.

It seemed a pleasant part of town, flat and festive, but pleasant. Most of the homes I passed would be in the $100,000-and-up class although there were a few smaller ones. At the end of the block where Wilson met Acacia there were two three-story apartment buildings facing each other.

The front door was open so I rang the bell and went right in. A short man in tartan trousers and a checked wool shirt bustled over to me, hand outstretched. He had a glass in the other hand.

'Don Kalvin,' he said.

'Victor Daniel,' I said.

'Vic,' he said. We shook hands. 'Swell of you to make it. Come on in and mingle.'

He led the way into a large living room.

'Here, dump that anywhere,' he said, referring to the briefcase, 'and I'll get you a drink. What's your poison?'

'Maybe later,' I said. The doorbell rang again.

'It's all go tonight,' he said, wheeling briskly away to answer it. 'Be right back. Don't start without me.'

I smiled at a couple of people who were smiling at me, then took a seat in one of the folding chairs that were set out in three rows against the far wall where a door led out to a porch and steps led down from it to the backyard. The yard lights were on to show off the Kalvin's Jacuzzi. I hate Jacuzzis. Water is bad enough when it's not doing anything but when it's scalding hot, bubbling and frothing it's impossible.

I looked around the room like a good detective. Lots of money and little taste is what I saw, a not uncommon combination in Southern California. Expensive Naugahyde sofas faced each other at right angles to an ornate stone and slate fireplace in which was a darling display of dried flowers. Heavy, octagonal end tables. Two tall chrome and smoked-glass floor lamps. Solid-looking ashtrays made from polished stone. Framed photographs, not pictures, on the walls, all slightly arty – long exposures of ribbons of light made by cars at night, a lone seagull at sunset, a close-up of a drop of water on a rose petal, that sort of thing.

A pretty woman wearing a silver jumpsuit with a pink heart sewn on approximately where hearts usually are and matching pink ballet slippers came over to me and said, 'Hi, I'm Dotty Kalvin, which number are you?'

'I don't have one,' I said, standing up politely. 'I'm the hired help.'

'Ohhh,' she said. 'Well hi, hired help. Drinkie?'

'Maybe later, thanks,' I said.

'Well Dotty is going to have a drinkie,' she said, turning and heading purposefully if a bit unsteadily towards a shelved alcove where the Kalvins kept their booze. The bar was already doing a steady business but it would be unfair to suggest there was a party feeling in the room, there wasn't, there were a lot of serious faces about and there were many people who were nursing fruit juice or a soft drink.

After a few more minutes Mr Kalvin checked his watch, said something to his wifie, who trotted off towards the front door, presumably to close it, then he raised his voice and suggested that everyone find a seat as they had better get going.

Mr Kalvin started by thanking everyone for coming. Then he asked everyone to stand up, introduce themselves and give their house or apartment address while Dotty checked off the numbers on a master list. It turned out there was at least one representative of every dwelling on Wilson between Acacia and Delmar except for three, which was pretty good, I thought. Then he recapped the reasons for the get-together although they were only too well known to most of the assembled multitude, he said. Two burglaries from homes, a mugging, three car thefts, a fire, two attempted muggings and at least one other attempted burglary from a house all in the last six months. And there might have been others he didn't know about. And he was only talking about their one street, a street of fifty-four houses and two apartments. He understood the adjoining streets were having similar crime waves, you'd have to call them. His double garage, which was also his workroom, had been broken into three days ago during the afternoon and all his power tools stolen and he had a lot of expensive power tools, right, Dotty?

'Right, Don,' said Dotty.

So he'd talked to the police about setting up a neighborhood watch. They said they'd be pleased to send someone along to talk to us about it but they couldn't do it for three weeks as they were booked up. He wasn't prepared to wait three weeks or three days. It was one angry man they saw standing up there. He'd called an expert, me, who he'd pay himself, no problem, to get things off the ground immediately.

'That's enough from me,' he said. 'OK, Vic, it's all yours.'

I moved my chair up beside the Kalvins' where I could be seen by one and all, opened up the briefcase and started my pitch. I told them who I was. I told them I'd been working in security for over ten years both independently and with various law-enforcement agencies, which was almost the truth. I told them to butt in with questions at any time. Then I let them have a few vital statistics from the Crime Commission report just as an attention-grabber, as the ad boys like to put it.

'About one in fifty,' I said, 'that's about the chance you have of being mugged. It's hard to say exactly but you've got more or less the same odds of being burgled in your home. Throw in your car and what can happen to it or to things in it and you're down to an even-money chance that at least one of those three will happen to you sometime. In fact I wouldn't be surprised if the odds aren't already worse than that.'

A murmur from the crowd. A few swear words from the crowd. A theatrical gasp from Dotty.

'Let's start with muggings. The word used to apply only to unarmed attacks, usually from behind, where the thief grabs the intended victim around the neck and squeezes until he or his pal has lifted the wallet or purse, but now mugging also includes personal robberies where the victim is threatened with and often injured by a weapon of some kind. A gun, a knife, a club, a bat, anything. A tire iron. Unfortunately the number of injuries occurring during muggings is going up sharply. Many muggings are inter-racial because it is safer – white people notoriously find it difficult to identify individual members of another race, whether it's black, Mexican, Chinese or farmers. The fact that those races seem to have the same trouble telling whites apart doesn't help much.

'Most muggers are youths, which might help us. Most aren't smart enough to take up a more elaborate form of crime. Most are from slums and most work surprisingly near where they live.'

'Why?' a man in the second row asked.

'No problems of transport, no feeling out of place in a strange part of town or looking out of place and thus being noticeable,' I said. 'Finally, there's been a change recently in the kind of places most muggings happen. Where it used to be streets and parks and parking lots, more and more now they happen in apartment buildings, either in the entrance or the elevators or in the halls. This is obviously safer for the mugger, he's got more time, no passers-by, no chance of a cop car cruising by. OK so far?'

'It's frightening,' one of the ladies said.

'You better believe it,' I said. 'And there's no way it's going to get better. Now. A word about what they call victimology before we move on. Without going into the psychology of the would-be victim, which is not my area . . .'

'Mine neither,' said Dotty. 'Sorry.'

'. . . there are obviously things you can do to increase or decrease the risks involved in living in a big city. Night time is more dangerous. Outside more dangerous than inside by three to one. Being old. Being alone. Carrying groceries or otherwise having your hands full. How you're dressed. Your race. Being foolish or negligent by leaving the keys in the car, flashing a wad of money buying something in a store. Wearing furs. Wearing jewelry. Talking to strangers, especially one or more youths. Buzzing in someone you don't know in an apartment building.'

'How many muggers do they catch?' one of the two black men in the room wanted to know.

'You're not going to like it,' I told him, 'but maybe, maybe five percent get a conviction of some kind.'

Whistles and headshakings.

'Does having more cops on the beat or in patrol cars help?' someone else asked.

'The short answer is no,' I said, 'unless you really saturate an area with police and keep them there. Some metropolitan areas have a ratio of one policeman to a thousand citizens, some four times that, and the crime statistics in both areas are still roughly the same, all other factors considered.'

'What about mace?' asked a short lady in a trouser suit who had brought her peke along. 'Stuff like that?'

'I don't know,' I had to admit. 'If I was young and foolish

and fit I might try a squirt and then make tracks but if I was old and tired or a woman I don't think I'd try it. Usually the stuff is in a purse or a pocket anyway and you're grabbed so quick it's already over. But you could try noise, especially outside. A lot of noise. Screaming. Maybe a whistle.'

'How about guns?' the other black man in the room asked.

'They go off,' I said. 'I don't think a law-abiding citizen should ever even think of walking around with one.'

'How about in your car or in the house?' he then asked.

'You tell me,' I said. 'I bet at least half the men in this room have got at least one somewhere.'

Silence.

'I will say this. Last study I read reported that of ten firearm deaths in the home, eight were suicides, one was one member of a family killing another, and most of the rest were accidental deaths. Only half of one per cent were of an intruder shot. However I can't deny having a gun around makes a lot of people, rightly or wrongly, feel safer. But, moving on to the next subject, guns won't help prevent the kind of break-ins you've been getting here in Wilson Crescent. The pattern in this sort of residential area has always been daytime robberies, by males fifteen to twenty-five, usually during school hours and often by schoolkids. Are there any schools near here?'

'About ten minutes thataway,' Mr Kalvin said.

'Close enough,' I said. 'What usually happens is this. The husband's out of the house working, the kids, if any, are at school themselves. The wife's out front gardening or picking oranges or slaving over a hot stove. A neatly dressed, nice-looking youth, probably white, in this area, nothing to be scared of, no huge rabid rapist, wanders by. He's maybe got a bottle of detergent in one hand or something innocuous like that. He's selling it or he wants to wash your windows or he wonders if you need a reliable gardening service a couple of times a week. The thing I must impress on you and what is hardest of all to accept is that he is innocent-looking, he's likable, so likable the victim often offers him a glass of water or gossips with him a minute – who wouldn't, a nice boy like that who could be one of your children's friends, just trying to make a little money? Maybe he's holding a piece of paper and is politely asking if you knew so and so who he thought was at this address. Got it? Innocent. And it's hard to say to a harmless-looking boy, beat it or I'll call a cop, especially when you're not sure he's up to anything wrong. Your immediate assumption should be, unfortunately, there is something wrong.

'After the initial contact, there's lots of ways it can develop. You offer him some odd job, he goes off around the corner to get his pal who's parked there out of sight. While you're talking with one boy out front or upstairs the other is around back filling up the trunk. If you're on your way out shopping and happen to mention it, he wanders off, waits til you go, comes back, cuts his way in through a screen. But he doesn't come out that way, it's too noticeable, he uses the door and in a minute or two you're minus a TV or two and the home computer and the hi-fi. Often the vehicle used is a van, often it says TV Repairs or Home Laundry on the side. It isn't hard to slide a lot of expensive loot into a laundry bag or laundry basket and what could look more innocent? The guy is young, remember, likable, whistling. Maybe he's got a Cable TV company T-shirt on. Or Arty's Woodworm Service While You Wait. So: you do not let anyone in or near your place for any reason whatsoever. A boy knocks and asks politely if he can use your phone as his car has broken down right outside – forget it. No good-looking youths for any reason whatsoever.'

A good-looking woman right in front of me sighed heavily and said, 'Oh, well,' which raised a chuckle.

I shuffled through my notes until I found the one I needed. I told them if they couldn't remember all the details, not to worry, I had made notes of all the main points and would hand out copies to everyone later. I did want them to think they were getting their money's worth, or in this case, Mr Kalvin's.

'Now we come to what you can do apart from being extremely leery about the youth of America. First. Protect your house. Proper locks, especially deadbolts on the main doors that can't be opened from the inside without a key because as I mentioned, seeing someone pass armloads of personal effects out a window is obviously suspicious. Windows should have proper locks and I don't mean a screen or one of those little catches, I mean the kind that turn with a sort of rollerskate key and drive a bolt into the window frame. A decent lock on the garage.'

'Now he tells me,' said Mr Kalvin ruefully.

'Second. Insurance, probably the cheapest, the best and often the only protection that works. Insure everything. Over-insure everything if you can as you only get the used value or the original value back. Insure your kitchen appliances. Gold, remember, and jewelry and art usually have to be insured separately. Money usually isn't insurable.

'Third.' I took out of the briefcase the small engraving tool I'd bought earlier at the hardware for $19.95. It looked like a dentist's drill and was the sort of thing jewelers used to engrave the backs of watches or the winners' names on trophies.

'A present from me to you,' I said. 'What you do with this is write your name on the back of everything stealable – hifis, TVs, radios, cameras, bicycles, boat engines. This procedure is recommended by the police as it does two things – it makes it possible to identify your goods and it is also illegal to sell items that have such identifying names on them or have had them sanded off – the police say it makes it easier for them to crack down on the middle-men. I personally am not sure it helps that much because if you want another hair-raising statistic, only about two percent of stolen goods are ever recovered and those mainly when the thief has been arrested in the act.'

That brought an angry murmur.

'I'll tell you something else,' I said. 'Unless goods worth five thousand dollars or more are stolen, chances are detectives won't even investigate. In some areas it's ten thousand dollars. Then you would get one visit from detectives and a follow-up one from a fingerprint expert, and that's all. So, basically, if it's gone it's gone for good.

'For those of you with expensive cars – and are there any other kind? – you might like to know there are several companies, one of which is Kar-Mark, that will mark identifying numbers on all your car windows. So when your Rolls is stolen, repainted and resold, it can still be identified as yours. And if someone wanders into a Rolls spare-parts division and asks for a half a dozen new windows, the salesman will be rightly suspicious. I know that a lot of garages now offer this service fairly inexpensively.

'Next. Setting up a neighborhood watch. First you need one person who's always or usually at home and it will be that person who contacts the police because that's the way they prefer it. You, being suspicious, call your spokesperson who immediately calls Lieutenant Ronald Isaacs, I'll give you the number, who is your local contact at the Sheriff's Department. I haven't talked to him yet because he was out earlier' (actually I'd forgotten) 'but I will as soon as you decide on one person and Mr Kalvin can pass the name on to me when he pays my modest fee.'

'Ha ha,' said Mr Kalvin.

'Next. Every home, every fence, every lamp post and tree has a large sign saying you belong to a neighborhood watch. I talked to a local sign store earlier and they can let you have them for fifty dollars a hundred, I've written their address down too, but if you fear I have some connection with that store, find one of your own. I've also left you some material from one of the private security companies that cover this area, you may find it interesting. Even if all of you don't want to go to the considerable expense, it might be worth your while to subsidize an occasional property just for the extra protection.'

'Not a bad idea,' someone said.

'Thank you,' I said. 'To wrap it up. You watch. You signpost saying that you are watching. A sign on the gate that says "Beware – Mad Dog" can't hurt either, especially if there are some traces that there actually is a mutt on the premises. If you care to, you mark. You insure heavily. You keep a list of serial numbers of your insured goods tucked away somewhere safe. You install proper locks. But most of all and most difficult of all, the first time some fresh-faced kid wanders your way, you say, excuse me, I left something on the stove, be right back, and you call your leader and she calls Lieutenant Isaacs. And that's about all from me, and about time, I hear you say. The rest, choosing your leader, delegating the various tasks, is up to you, unless there are any questions.'

'Those little round things some doors have to see through,' said a lady.

'Judas windows,' said another.

'Good,' I said. 'Cheap, easy to install. Just beware the likable, fresh-faced youth who comes around out of nowhere offering to install one for you.'

I shook a hand or two, left all the material I'd promised, then left them if not laughing, at least buzzing.

Another day, another $200. Well, I had worked for it, what I reported here were just the outlines, it took over two hours to go through it in detail at the Kalvins'. I hoped it would help. It's surprising how difficult it can be sometimes to get people to beware of other members of their own species.

On the way home, wouldn't you know, I got mugged.

CHAPTER EIGHT

As it wasn't all that late, a little after ten, I stopped at the Two-Two-Two on the way home for some needed and well-earned alcoholic refreshment. You might not know it but it's a tiring business performing, one might even say, starring, for hours in front of a critical first-night audience.

So I had a couple of brandy and gingers there then popped over to the Corner Bar and put my initials on the blackboard, which was what you did when you wanted a game of pool and the table was in use. When your turn came you put in the fifty cents and played the last winner. A hefty gal known as Baby was on a run when I got to the table; I soon took care of Baby with a little help from a fluky bank shot. I like bars. Neighborhood bars, hotel bars, Mexican bars, downtown bars, small-town bars, piano bars and jazz joints. I like English pubs and Irish bars and French cafés although I've never been in a real one and probably never will; hell, I even like airport bars.

I left the Corner Bar about eleven thirty and was standing there minding my business, wondering idly whether to visit the Three Jacks or the Cloverleaf next, when it happened. The first hit was right in the small of my back; I went down, head first, half on the sidewalk, half in the street. I was trying to roll over when I got clipped again, on the shoulder, then on the arm. I got a glimpse of an angry red face under a baseball cap, then a close-up of a golf club, a wood. It caught me right on the chin and I started losing it. I heard someone shouting at me to stay out of it. Then whoever it was stepped closer and began putting the boot in – the back, the face, the gut. Enough's enough, I thought. Now you've made me mad, I thought. Smiling, I closed my eyes and went to sleep.

When I came to the first thing I saw was a brick. It was in the middle of a lot more bricks. They were nice bricks, brick-colored, cemented neatly together to form what is called a wall. By slowly moving my eyeballs I discovered I was lying on my side in the alley next to the Corner Bar. It was comfortable there, maybe I'd stay a while. I could have the kindly barman make a hole in the wall right in front of my face and serve me through it. My nose was bleeding and one of my eyes was watering, at least I hoped it was water. My back was on fire, my left arm numb, and for a while I was afraid to try moving anything important, like my mouth.

Well, when the going gets tough, the tough get going, and after a while I got going too, after a while. Before long I was on my knees, then I was walking, sort of, down the alley. Turn right. Lean against the car for a spell. I loved my car, I realized suddenly. I had always ridiculed it. I loved my Nash. I still had my keys and my wallet so maybe I hadn't been mugged after all but merely whupped and left out in the cold to die, like old Eskimos.

I didn't know where I was going but my car did. I didn't want to go home to Mother because that's all she needed, blood as well as never-ending fluff on our new carpet, to say nothing of me. A hospital wouldn't have been a bad idea but the car had a better one – Evonne's.

When she finally answered her door I was slumped on the back porch looking up at the night sky. I loved the night sky. Evonne wanted to know just what I thought I was doing there in the middle of the night.

'Got any aspirin?' I said bravely.

She took a closer look. Then she said something short and unladylike but all of the ladies I know say it all the time now. Then, with a little help from her, I crawled inside, through the small living room, down the hall, into the bathroom and up on the toilet seat, from where I grinned at my darling.

'My hero,' she said a mite scornfully, or sarcastically, if

you will, her hands on her hips, looking down at me. 'Home from the wars, are we? Lose a fight with a Mack truck, did we?'

I smiled amiably at her, despite her heartless behavior. Then, with me directing, she got to work. Pain pills. Cold water. More cold water. Freezing water. Butterfly bandages on the forehead. Nose taped so tightly the tears came. Icy cold freezing water. I hate cold water. Sponge. Some sort of liniment. Warm sheets. Warm Evonne next to me, in her outsize waterbed. I hate waterbeds, they're so Californian and every time you try and snuggle a little closer to a girl in one you've got to wait for a favorable tide.

'Go to sleep,' Evonne said crossly.

Well, I like that. I'm the one who's dying and she's cross. It was ironic, though, a supremely ironic moment – it was the first time I'd ever been in her bed and I was bashed up so badly I couldn't have done any of those fun things people do in beds even if she'd let me. Which, needless to say, she didn't, in about ten seconds she callously went off to slumberland. Truly did Liberace once remark to a drinking buddy, 'Dames is grief', to which his buddy replied, 'Time's a thief'. I like Liberace's line best, although it's a tough choice.

Came the dawn. Came the aches and pains, came the bruises – yellow, purple and Indian brown. Came the sweats. Came my sweet with pain pills and a mug of tea, all dressed and ready to go to work. One of her eyebrows had been drawn on unevenly.

'Leave the key under the pot on the left when you go,' she said.

'Yes, dear,' I said meekly.

She started rummaging through my pants pockets.

'The money's in the wallet, babe,' I said.

'Don't be stupid,' she said. 'Your car's blocking mine. I need the keys.'

'Probably still in it,' I said.

She flounced out; a minute later I heard her doing her best to strip my gears as she tried to find reverse. She came back in with a piece of paper from a scratch pad which she put down on the bedside table.

'Doctor Asami. He's just down the street if you need him.'

'Nah,' I said. 'I'm O K, I'll be out of here by noon. Thanks for everything. You done good. I wasn't really trying to get into your bed. I mean, I was, but not this way. Maybe just a little.'

'You big palooka,' she said. 'In fact, you enormous palooka.' She bent down and gave me a quick kiss – raspberry, my favorite.

She left; I dozed, visions of an angry red-faced golfer with an Irish accent dancing in my head, one Mr 'Gillespie' I could only presume. I mean I didn't have so many enemies I didn't know who they were. In fact I only had one regular, Mick the prick, and he was about as Irish as Mohammed Ali and roughly the same color. I would have to find Mr Gillespie and have a word with him. He had found me without too much trouble and I had even less trouble figuring out how – he gets my name and description from his wife one way or another, probably the other. He looks me up in the phone book and gives me a tinkle, to see if I'm in. My mom helpfully says no, but she knows where I am, because I always leave an address and phone number when I go out at night in case Feeb needs it for anything. Inflamed by the demon rum, no doubt, he follows me from the Kalvins' until he catches me alone, standing on the corner waiting for the parade.

I felt a touch better when I woke up for the second time later that morning, well enough to get dressed. I even rinsed my tea mug. Then I called Mom, who sounded fine, and told her her naughty boy, battered but unbowed, was on his way home after a night on the tiles. Then I called Meg, a florist I knew over on Chelsea Drive, and arranged to have some roses delivered to Evonne where she worked as (1) where she worked was within Meg's delivery area and (2) it would give the other secretaries something to gossip about. Then I departed, leaving the door key where I was supposed to, under the flower pot on the left, the first place a sneak thief would look.

At home I took a couple of real pain pills, Demerols, had a glass of buttermilk and betook myself back to bed where, except for a bite of supper, I remained until late the following morning, dozing and reading some old Max Brand Westerns my mother must have smuggled into the house sometime when I wasn't looking. I also came up with a few ideas of how to locate Mr Gillespie and a few more about what to do to him when I did find him. Evonne called, we had the kind of conversation I'm best at, one about nothing at all.

Before going into work Wednesday I rebandaged my nose and had my back checked out by an osteopath I went to once in a while whose office was near mine, Larry, an earnest young chap who was mostly beard. He asked me the usual searching personal question – cash or insurance – then cracked my neck, stretched my vertebrae and had his assistant Mary-Lynn give me some deep heat right in the small of the back.

At the office I remembered to call Lieutenant Ronald Isaacs at the sheriff's station serving Mr Kalvin's neighborhood and we chewed the fat for a while. And I tried Art Feldman in case he'd come back early but he was still lost in the rough somewhere. Then I went through the mail, of which the most interesting item was a note from my ever-hopeful dentist saying it was time for my six-monthly check-up and would I please phone for an appointment. I set up Betsy, then had a phone call from Sara the punk poet, Sara with the Technicolor hair and three earrings in one lobe and none in the other.

'What's up, Shorty?' she wanted to know. 'What's been goin' down? Glad I'm back?'

'Thrilled,' I said. 'Now beat it, I'm busy.'

'Ha ha,' she said. 'That'll be the day. You're probably playing some kid's game on that dumb computer.'

'Computers are not dumb,' I said. 'People are dumb. And I am not playing a kid's game, I happen to be playing an extremely difficult adult search and destroy game called "Attack on Mongo".'

'Listen,' she said. 'I'm bored. You got anything for me to do?'

'No,' I said. 'Go write some more unspeakable poetry.' I hung up. What a twerp. Five foot nothing of skinny punk twerp.

While I was on the phone I'd noticed a worried-looking individual walk past my window a couple of times and sneak a quick peek in. He must have finally made up his mind because the next time he passed he actually stopped at the door, read the sign on it – 'V. Daniel – Investigations', it said, followed by my office hours and office and home phone numbers, then he came in and introduced himself.

'Jonathan Lubinski,' he said, handing me his card.

'Victor Daniel,' I said, taking it. 'Lubinski, Lubinski and Levi, Family Jewelers for over Twenty Years', it read. I knew the store although I'd never been in it. It was right across the street from Mrs Martel's stationery store and the post office I used.

We shook hands, we sat down. I switched Betsy off and looked attentive. Mr Lubinski was a slender gentleman in his sixties with gold-framed glasses, wearing a well-cut dark-green suit a shade too tight showing plenty of large, round cufflinks that looked like gold-plated watch movements. Slim tie and gold tiepin. Highly polished black loafers with tassels. Cream-colored shirt.

'What can I do for you, sir?' I asked him.

'I don't quite know,' he said. With his Middle European accent the 'quite' came out more like 'k'vite'. 'Yesterday I had a visit from a man, a gangster, a Mafia, a hoodlum, a nothing. More gold on him than me even.' He smiled, showing perfect teeth. I bet he never needed reminders from his dentist.

'Did he give you a name?'

'Fat chance.'

'What did he look like?'

'A hoodlum! Italian. Black hair. Sheepskin jacket. Fake suntan.'

'Big?'

He shrugged. 'To me, big. To you, not so big.'

'So what did he want?'

'It turns out he wants to sell us gold.'

'How much?'

'Lots.'

'For how much?'

'Two-fifty,' said Mr Lubinski.

'How much is that in dollars?' I said.

'It is in dollars,' he said. 'Two hundred and fifty US dollars an ounce. Yesterday the New York Comex current closed at three hundred and forty-two dollars. And twenty cents.'

'Well, the price is right,' I said.

'And that's all that is,' Mr Lubinski said. 'At that price it has to be stolen or smuggled. I said, did he know there were laws specifically designed to prevent such a sale? Such as all wholesalers have to buy precious metals from registered brokers? Such as, every ounce must be accounted for in our annual inventories and sales? Or else automatic loss of trading license, or else a fine as well, or else, half the time, jail as well? Then what do you think he said?'

'I don't know,' I said.

'He said, "That's your problem, Mr Lubinski." And that is when Mr Lubinski started getting worried.'

'How much does he want you to take?'

'Four lots of ten thousand dollars' worth, for starters,' Mr

Lubinski said, patting his pockets. 'Sometimes I wish I still smoked. I could use a smoke. I could use a drink. I had a drink last night – in fact, many. My wife wanted to know if it was another woman. I said I only wished it was.'

'In what form would the gold be?'

'He didn't say yet but that much, it has to be bars or parts of bars. It ain't going to be charm bracelets.'

I had to laugh.

'So you think it's funny, eh? I told him Lubinski, Lubinski and Levi couldn't use all that much anyway, and he says, "You got friends, don't you?" So I says, "Listen, tell you what, with Lubinski, Lubinski and Levi it is impossible, take my word, but why don't you try that madman Salomen over on Victory, that thief, he'll do business with you like that, with the snap of a finger, that cheap momzer."

'"So forget it," he says. "My employer has decided to do business with Lubinski, Lubinski and Levi, and believe me, Mr Lubinski, I like to keep my employer happy. He's terrible when he becomes annoyed, simply terrible. Like an animal," he says, "Violent. Crazed. Why, once I saw him hit a man with an ash can, an elderly gent like you, too. Then he had a truck full of two tons of sand driven right through the man's store front, imagine." Well, I could imagine, all right, and that's when I started really getting worried instead of just worried. So then he shakes hands politely and off he goes, he doesn't even bother telling me not to go to the police – what am I, totally insane? But Lubinski has to do something, and fast. I thought about selling out and moving to Israel to visit my trees but you never heard my wife on the subject of Israel. I thought about selling out and moving to Israel without my wife. So I was in the paper store across from me and Mrs Martel says, "What's by you, Mr Lubinski?", only she calls me Solly as we're old friends, "You look like you got problems."

'"Problems," I said. "I wish that was all I had. What I got

is a catastrophe." "So go see my good friend and valued customer Mr Victor Daniel," she says with a wink. "He's good at things like that." It couldn't hurt, I tell her, worse than it does now, so here I am.'

'Fine woman, Mrs Martel,' I said.

'Sally,' Mr Lubinski said, a hint of longing or perhaps memory in his voice. 'Together we're Sally and Solly.'

'Who's the other Mr Lubinski?' I asked him.

'My cousin Nate. My mother's sister's boy.'

'And Mr Levi?'

'With the angels, God bless that wonderful man.'

'Does your cousin know what happened?'

'Not yet and please God he shouldn't have to,' said Mr Lubinski. 'Now let me ask you a question – what do we do now?'

'Let me have a think,' I said. 'When's that guy coming back, did he say?'

'Saturday morning, bright and early, is what he said.'

I stood up. 'All right. I'll give you a call when I've worked something out. And don't worry, with your brains and my muscle we should be able to handle one Italian errand boy.'

'It's the animal, thank you, his employer, I'm worried about,' said Mr Lubinski, getting up as well. 'Listen, son, you want something on account?'

'Next time,' I said, and walked him the few steps to the door.

'Next time yourself, don't forget to duck,' he said over his shoulder as he walked away, the only comment he made at all about my battered visage.

I was just thinking about closing up, having some lunch, and maybe taking a long stroll to work out some of the stiffness and also have a ponder about the venerable firm of Lubinski, Lubinski and Levi when the phone rang. It was a very worried Ricky.

'Chico never came home last night,' he said. 'I waited all

night at his place, I just got to the office. I don't like it. I hate to bother you but I can't go to the police or even my own department as he's an illegal alien illegally living on government land and I put him there.'

'Maybe he just slept out, did he ever do that?'

'Never,' said Ricky positively. 'Never once, since his days in the mountains. Anyway, with what? He's got no sleeping bag, his blankets are on the bed, all his things are still here, and it's January, man, it gets cold at night. I don't like it.'

I didn't like it a hell of a lot myself. I liked it as little as I liked people who asked me what the weather was like up there, which was not at all in the slightest.

CHAPTER NINE

I met Ricky later that afternoon, as arranged, in Parson's Crossing, after he was done work for the day, and once again we bumped and slid our way up the old logging road to the top of the rise where we'd stopped before. Then, after he had donned his all-purpose survival belt again, we finished the trip on foot.

The cabin looked and felt the same, there were no obvious omens of disaster, no circling vultures or two-headed calves being born or cackling witches. Or maybe there just wasn't enough of the mystic in me. I went inside, leaving the door open to get a little light on the scene while Ricky prowled around outside looking for clues or merely burning off some of his worry-inspired excess energy.

When my eyes became accustomed to the comparative gloom I took a long, careful look around although I didn't know what I was looking for, nor did I know if there was anything there to look for or if I would recognize it when I saw it. It does get complicated, my line of work. However, good habits are their own reward, as an old cellmate used to say. Chico's bedding was still there, as Ricky had said. So was his cold-weather gear, a sort of sweater coat made of heavy, raw wool I'd noticed on the last visit. Then I spied with my little eye something I'd also noticed before but it hadn't sunk in – hanging from a nail on the wall, beside the fireplace, among Chico's dried and drying herb collection, was one large sprig of a herb whose primary function wasn't to be sprinkled into beef goulash or eggs maryland. This one you smoked. People claimed that after a few puffs you giggled a lot and developed an inordinate hunger for anything at all you could scrounge including dry muesli or warm pickle juice.

So I gave the sprig a sniff and a feel – it was drying but still resinous, i.e. fairly fresh. I went back outside and sat on the tree stump that was holding the door open til Ricky wandered by a few minutes later.

'See anything?' I asked him.

He shook his head. 'You?'

'Yep.' I handed him my discovery. He crushed a few leaves and smelled them.

'Weed,' he said.

'Yep,' I said. 'You bring it for him?'

'No,' he said. 'Never.'

'Ellena?'

'Not a chance. She didn't think it was good for him. She hates the stuff. But Chico was always growing it or finding it somewhere.'

'A pretty problem, then, Señor Watson,' I said. 'Let us reflect a minute. Did he grow it around here?'

'No,' said Señor Watson. 'Not around here. I covered a mile, maybe a mile and a half, all around here yesterday looking for him. Anyway, it needs direct sunlight and there's too much cover here. And along the roads would be too obvious.'

'How about wild?'

'No,' he said again. 'Not in this neck of woods. Anyway, this isn't wild. It's cultivated. It's strong shit, man. Maybe he gets it from that park.'

'I can find out,' I said, picking a bit of bark off the tree stump. 'I've got to call the animal lady anyway. I should have done it before, about replacing those bloody sheep. But from what she told me about the place and how uptight they are I don't think it's a likely source of full-grown pot plants. Someone there may have their little stash hidden away for emergencies but not au naturel, so to speak. So who else? Who else does he know?'

Ricky shrugged restlessly. 'No one, hombre.'

I had a thought. 'How about the fire-watcher, didn't you say you took him up there once? If I had to live all alone up a tower in the middle of a jungle I'd probably smoke dope, too. Did Chico ever go back there?'

'I can find out easy,' Ricky said. 'He's got a radio phone.'

'Can we visit him instead?'

'Sure, but why?'

'Just for fun,' I said. 'I've never been up in one of those things.' And I wasn't looking forward to the first time, either. I suffer badly from vertigo, so much so I can't even sit up in the balcony of a movie house anymore even if I'm lucky enough to be with the kind of girl who would sit in the balcony with me in the first place. I did manage to fly once, but never again. And I've never forgiven, nor do I ever intend to forgive, that nerd Sara for forcing me into it that one horrible time.

'So let's do it now,' Ricky said.

'Is it far?'

'As the crow flies, no, but we got to go around, so maybe three quarters of an hour. There'll be plenty of light left if we step on it.'

'Anda,' I said. 'Mush, you huskies.' I hung Chico's weed back on the wall upside down as I'd found it, took a last look around, then got out of there and followed mi amigo back to the Wagoneer. I didn't think I'd ever be back. But I was wrong.

We had to retrace our route almost back to the forestry office in order to pick up the road we wanted, so we stopped off to phone from Ricky's office. He called Ellena to fill her in, then I started tracking down Olivia, the keeper of the flock.

I finally got through to her in the canteen. She was eating the vegetarian plate, she told me. I was in Parson's Crossing, I told her, eating a stale Mars Bar I'd just bought at Mae's dinette.

Then I told her, with suitable modesty, that I'd solved the case of the missing mutton. Without going into all the petty details (and one or two of the important ones) I informed her they had been taken by a troubled soul who had been camping nearby, that I had apprehended him, that it wouldn't happen again, that although the original animals were no longer alive I was empowered to cover any costs involved in replacing them. I suggested she call Emile Who Talked to God to see if he had any suitable animals. If he did, and as he owed me one, he woud let her have them cheap and that saving could be passed along to the Troubled Soul who believe me had enough problems without paying top dollar for five Suffolks. If she agreed not to prosecute him I would show my gratitude by reducing my already ludicrously low fee to say a token twenty bucks and gas. Plus a free ticket for sometime in the future for admission to Wonderland Park for a family of three. Make that three and a half. Finally, I would agree to cancel my impending lawsuit against her and Wonderland Park for the savage and unwarranted attack made on me by that South American carnivore.

'Done,' Olivia said, laughing. 'Settled out of court. Would that family be your family?'

'No,' I said, 'a friend's.'

'Why don't you come too?' she said. 'Then you can tell me all the bits of the story you left out hoping I wouldn't notice.'

'Done,' I said. 'To make it easier, tell Emile I'll pay him directly for the sheep, then you won't have to lay out anything.'

'You got it,' she said.

I asked her then about dope smoking among the staff at the park. When she hedged a trifle, I told her it could be important so she allowed that from time to time of an evening she and the dolphin gal shared a peaceful pipe of hash, but as far as she knew that was it as far as drugs went. I thanked her and hung up.

Ricky and I went by Tommy's office on our way out; he was sitting with his feet up on the desk looking through a gun catalogue. Ricky let out a derisive whistle of admiration when he saw Tommy's fancy new snakeskin boots.

'Ay yi yi,' he said. 'What did you do, roll a pimp?'

Tommy grinned all over his freckled face. Then he wagged a finger at his buddy. 'You be careful with that re-al-tor,' he said. 'Behind that mean exterior there could lurk a mean interior.'

As soon as I realized the realtor he was talking about was me, as that's what Ricky had told him I was on our last trip, I gave him a grin right back, my boyish one. It didn't seem to impress him much.

There were three cars parked outside along with the two Wagoneers. One of them was a low-slung Nipponese hatchback with wire radials.

'Nice wheels,' I said as we passed it.

'Tommy's,' Ricky said. 'Lucky bastard.'

'Why lucky?'

'His brother got it for him. He's in some part of the business, buying or selling, I dunno, he's always away. It was one of those repos sent up for auction. What they do is strip it, give it a terrible paint job, pour some guck over the engine because people who don't know anything about cars always think that if the engine's clean it means the owner has really looked after it. Then you buy it cheap, shove all the extras back in it, strip the lousy paintwork off, clean up the interior and you've got yourself fancy wheels for nada, man.'

'Ain't some people dishonest,' I said, shaking my head. 'Where does your pal live, near you?' We got into Ricky's Jeep and took off.

'At his brother's, in Sherman Oaks. We've been there a couple of times for barbecues. Nice place.'

We continued with the small talk more or less deliberately to stop ourselves thinking about more serious things until we turned off on to another one of those logging roads that was so bumpy all a guy could do was hang on and swear, him in Spanish, me in American.

It was just on five thirty when the road got so bad we had to park. We spent the next twenty minutes walking straight up the side of a cliff. Luckily I was in pretty good shape that year, I was bowling a few frames with John D. at the Valley Bowl once a month or so and there was all that walking from the Corner Bar to the Two-Two-Two, which were a good hundred yards apart. But my back was still tender and my legs sore from having been used for driving practice, so I wasn't sorry when we arrived at the foot of the fire tower.

It was built the way you would build a three-sided tower out of matchsticks, triangles of logs laid on top of each other with ladders made of wood sort of zig-zagging up the middle. On the top was a square wooden watchtower resting on a platform. Ricky kindly let me get my breath back while he exchanged shouted insults with the inhabitant, who had seen us coming and was leaning out of one of the windows.

Then, up we went. It wasn't too bad for the first few rungs, then I had to close my eyes, opening them only when we had to shift to the next ladder and then being careful to stay focused on something very close to me, like my hands or the peeled wood of the ladder. On the third ladder I was sick. On the fifth ladder I almost lost it completely and had to hang on until the whirling and falling sensations stopped. It all sounds a bit old-maidish, I know, a man my size coming down with the vapors, but I was a good fifty feet up by then. On the sixth ladder I was sick. When I managed the seventh and final ladder, the hatch above it was open and a smiling, bearded flower-child helped me through it. The first thing I saw was a large sign that said 'Welcome To Heaven. Glad You Made It'. The next thing I saw was a can of Coors which the beard was holding out to me. It was ice cold and as good as a Coors can ever be, which is fair. Ricky, who was

78

bringing up the rear, joined us soon thereafter and made the introductions.

'Lucky, Vic. Vic, Lucky.' Lucky gave me two high fives, then two low fives. He was a short, skinny, hairy lad in his twenties attired in light-blue jeans which some loving hand had flared at the bottoms and then decorated with embroidered flowers. I found out later the loving hand was his; when he had nothing to do, which was most of the time, he said, he had himself a toot and got out the sewing basket.

Lucky had made himself comfortable in his home away from home. His cabin reminded me of Chico's, being roughly the same size and also made of wood, but Lucky had a bottled-gas fridge and bottled-gas camper's stove instead of a fireplace. On the ceiling was a beautifully stitched patchwork quilt, also Lucky's work, he told me diffidently. When I took a closer look I saw he'd hidden among the patchwork the outlines of various animals.

There were large windows in each of the four walls, with wooden shutters that closed from the inside. The rest of the wall space was covered with maps and charts of the local flora and fauna, also mushrooms, trees, birds and fishes. Prominent also, needless to say, were the tools of his trade — a huge pair of binoculars on a swivel mount that was calibrated in degrees, also a telescope on its tripod and a large radio telephone. When I asked him how they got all the equipment and supplies up to Heaven he smiled and pointed out one of the windows where a couple of ropes were neatly tied off.

'Windlass,' he said. He consulted a mammoth chronometer he wore on one wrist, said, 'Hang on', then sat on a stool, took a reading through the binoculars, made a note in a ledger, shifted the alignment a trifle, took another reading, then made a second note. He also took a careful look out of every window in turn without the binoculars.

'All quiet on the Western Front,' he said. He stooped down

suddenly and picked up a loose bit of thread which he rolled up in his fingers and tucked away in a pocket.

After a while I found I could look out the windows if I didn't get too close to them so I took a turn at the binoculars, being careful not to disturb their setting although Lucky told me it didn't matter, with a flick o' the wrist he could easily re-set them. And the view was amazing, if slightly monotonous, mile after mile of woodland, forest and hills, all in shades of green and brown, highlighted here and there by the last of the late afternoon sun. I don't know what power those binoculars were but they were about a foot long and the detail they picked up was surprising to a landlubber like me.

I asked Lucky if he remembered Chico's visit.

'Surely,' he said, sprinkling just a soupçon of chocolate into the coffee he was making for us. 'A sweet man in a broken body. Ricky said the fuzz back where they came from poured enough juice through him to light up a small town. All in all, I think I'll stay up here in Heaven, thanks. In a storm it's insanely beautiful.'

'Did Chico ever come back?'

'Nope, not when I was here, anyway. And Freddy would have mentioned it, I mean, how many visitors do we get?'

'Who's Freddy?'

'I do six weeks up, then one down,' Lucky said, stirring his concoction cautiously. 'Then comes the Fred.'

'Ever give Chico any dope, Lucky?' Ricky asked him. 'Good home-grown, not cleaned yet?'

'Never had any good home-grown up here that wasn't clean,' he said. 'Why bother? And the Fred never touches the stuff. He gets off on pink gin, gin and angostura bitters.' He shuddered at the very thought.

'What did Chico do the time he was here?' I asked them both.

'Looked out the windows through the glasses,' said Lucky, swooping on another bit of thread. 'Couldn't drag him away, right, Ricardo?'

Ricardo nodded. I said, 'Good coffee,' although I don't really like anything in my coffee but coffee and especially not chocolate or cinnamon. Lucky looked pleased. I was interested in his way of life. I too had my dreams of getting away from it all as I have perhaps already mentioned several dozen times, but here was someone who was not only getting away from it all, he was being paid for it. So I asked him what else he did besides sew and fire watch. It turned out his days were fuller than he'd first let on as he had a small sideline going with the Weather Bureau and every four hours took readings of the barometric pressure and the outside temperature, noted the type and amount of cloud cover, then hoisted himself up on the roof to measure the rainfall, if any, and also the prevailing wind speed and direction. Then he owned up he also belonged to the Audubon Society plus the Sierra Club and wrote the occasional piece for them on matters of general interest such as the feeding habits of the lesser spotted tit – his words, not mine.

'It's a long way to go for a beer of an evening though,' I remarked at some stage.

'You better believe it,' he said. 'You're looking at an alcoholic, so the farther the better.' Then he showed me a color photo of a desolate, treeless mountain top; some timber company had been through and cut everything with branches, it was a real-estate nightmare that looked like something left over after WWIII.

'Lucky Mountain,' he said with great pride. 'And one day it will be mine all mine. Have you any idea what it will be like in twenty years when the new growth hides all that shit?'

I said I didn't.

'Listen,' he said, striding around excitedly. He spotted yet another loose thread and bent to pick it up. 'I live free, or almost free, don't need many clothes and I make most of those, so almost all my not ungenerous salary is going into buying Lucky Mountain, now known only as MM-22-Six on a logging map, and, say, ten grand a year over fifteen years will buy you a lot of mountain, especially when it looks like this.' He put the photograph away carefully. 'You'll have to come up and visit me there sometime,' he said.

'Love to,' I said. 'Where is it?'

'Alberta, roughly,' he said with a grin.

'That'll make it easy to find,' I said.

I finished my coffee like a good boy, refused seconds, and said we had to be on our way, unfortunately.

'So what's it all about?' Lucky asked us as he pulled up the hatch in the floor. 'Something happen to Chico?'

'Roughly,' I said. He grinned again, or I thought he did. It was hard to tell through all that beard.

Going down was easier than going up only because I knew in advance this time it was a one-way trip, but that did not make it fun. I asked my shrink pal Art once where fear of heights comes from but I don't remember what his answer was. Probably, call my secretary for an appointment. Lucky came down with us to see us off, hot-dogging it by sliding down the ladders using only his hands.

After Ricky and I had bumped our way out to the main road, I asked him if he'd mind pulling over at some suitable spot for a minute. He looked at me inquiringly but did so. After he shut the motor off, he asked me,

'Que pasa, amigo?'

'I'll tell you what's passing, amigo,' I said, shaking my head sadly. 'Beware of likable, honest-looking, fresh-faced kids.'

CHAPTER TEN

There are no hours for someone in my line of work, or rather, no fixed hours, although I do try to be in the office when the sign on the door says I should be. But there's no sense at all in being your own boss if you can't show up late or go home early or take the day off and go fishing from time to time. To balance this apparent freedom are the times I have to work late or on weekends or throughout National Dog Week and other major holidays.

So that night after parting with a worried Ricky and driving home, I decided that I would put in some late work. After smothered pork chops and crinkle-cut french fries with Mom, I donned my thinking clothes, took myself over to the Corner Bar, installed myself in the back booth, ordered up the usual, and thought. Well, thinking's work, isn't it? It is for me.

After twenty minutes of heavy rumination, I got some change from the waitress Cherie and headed for the phone by the men's room. The out-of-town-information operator got me the number I wanted and after depositing most of the change I was connected to my party, ex-Sheriff Gutes, of Modesto, CA. I'd never met the man but I'd talked to him on the phone some months ago and he'd been helpful then. I wasn't sure he'd remember me but I needn't have worried.

'Of course,' he said. 'Victor Daniel. You called me last May about Dev Devlin. Hang on til I turn that Goddamned TV down.' I hung on. 'What finally happened on that?' he asked when he came back.

'Oh, it all worked out,' I told him. 'Nam screwed him up a bit, that was all.'

'He's not the only one,' Sheriff Gutes said. 'So what can I do for you this time?'

'You ever run across a husband and wife name of De-Marco, they have a farm of some kind outside your fine burg?'

'Nope, but I could track 'em down with no problem.'

'Good,' I said. 'Do you think you could use your wiles and find out where their sons are without them getting suspicious?'

'I reckon I got enough wiles left for that, sure.'

'One called Thomas, L.L., or Tommy, and a second one are supposed to be sharing a house down here in Sherman Oaks, if that helps,' I said.

'Got a good reason why I should take my wiles out of mothballs?' the old gent asked.

'Sure do,' I said.

There was a pause, then a chuckle from Mr Gutes.

'Give me a number and I'll get back to you,' he said. 'Shouldn't take long.'

I read off the number from the dial, hung up, and watched two guys shoot bad eight-ball for a few minutes. Then Mr Gutes called back.

'One son only, name of Thomas, L.L., like you said, also one daughter. You sure you got the right folks?'

'Now I'm positive,' I said. 'If you don't mind me asking an old dog to reveal his trade secrets, how'd you do it?'

He chuckled again. 'You probably don't know the local American Legion here is conducting a membership drive and therefore trying to contact all Vets in the area.'

'No, I didn't know that, nor do I believe it,' I said. 'But what if Thomas isn't a Vet?'

'He isn't,' said Mr Gutes. Then, in a falsetto lady's voice, he said. '"Oh, but we've only got Tommy and he's never been in the service. There's Cathy-Sue, but she's married and living in New York." If you call that living.'

'You old smoothie,' I said. 'Many thanks.'

'Glad I could help,' he said. 'Drop by, son, if you're ever by this way. I'm usually home, damn it.'

I said I would, thanked him again, sat down and ordered another brandy and ginger. I was so pleased I tipped Cherie fifty cents instead of my usual quarter. She pretended to reel with the shock.

There were several other ways I could have found out about Tommy's non-existent brother, of course. If you own property you're automatically down on more records than Bing Crosby and most of those are open to the public, but it is always gratifying to come up with needed information without having to leave the bar you're in. It might be considered the mark of the true professional.

Logic. What can one say about logic? I do not care for it overmuch but it can be helpful:

1. Chico was missing, presumed, by me at least, dead.

2. There was in all probability a serious intention behind his death because . . .

3. . . . . it was unlikely there was a non-serious intention, such as a domestic flare-up, a car accident, a sudden bar quarrel or a mugging, given his isolated circumstances.

4. It was likely that the reason had something to do with money, serious money, either in the making of it or the protecting of how it was made.

5. There is serious money in growing dope. According to a recent article I'd read somewhere, not my dentist's waiting room, roughly one (1) million acres of the National Forest system were being used by marijuana growers. The largest single area was up north in Humboldt, Trinity and Mendocino countries, insiders call it the Emerald Triangle. North Carolina, Arkansas, Florida and Missouri were the other main problem areas. The growers commonly protected their plantations with guns, boobytraps, dogs, even mines. The Forest Service workers were not as yet allowed to carry

firearms so they had to depend on outside law-enforcement agencies to protect them, not a helpful state of affairs when you're being shot at, bombed and mined. Finally, it might be remembered that there are other forests in America aside from National Forests.

6. Chico had some dope he didn't grow himself.

7. Nor could we find anyone who gave it to him or sold it to him, if he even had money.

8. I postulated therefore that he had stolen it from someone, and almost surely, someone who was growing it.

9. I further postulated from the above that, as Chico had been down to his last sprig, which is a time of great fear and paranoia for the habitual user – for further research in this area witness my landlord's panic when his cookie jar runs low – he'd been off stealing some more, had been detected and killed, either accidentally or on purpose.

10. Therefore Chico, in his wanderings, had either stumbled across – or, more likely, gone looking for – a pot plantation which he had seen through the binoculars up in the fire tower, a patch of green he recognized, a truck, some movement that made him curious.

11. Now, serious money does not come from one pot plant or two or three, it comes from a couple of hundred, at least. It comes from a veritable plantation, it comes from a sizable tract of land.

12. The foresty land north of Wonderland Park was under the direct surveillance of two rangers, Tommy and Ricky.

13. Rule out Ricky and his territory.

14. That left Tommy and his.

15. Ricky mentioned he knew, if not every tree in his section, almost every one. I assumed Tommy had similar knowledge. Several hundred pot plants up to five feet tall can't be grown, weeded, sprayed, picked back, debugged, harvested and whatever in complete secrecy, especially in an area that's regularly patrolled and is known intimately by an expert.

Even if the patch wasn't visible from a road there would still be tire tracks and other signs of regular visitations.

16. Therefore, Tommy was involved. Therefore Tommy was on the take somehow.

17. Further proof of 16: Baby had new shoes, or more precisely, snakeskin boots, an expensive set of wheels and a costly house to live in – the last two supposedly courtesy of a brother who was not only never home, as Ricky had mentioned, but non-existent.

18. Final, conclusive proof of 16: Tommy was young, fresh-faced, innocent-looking, likable and seemingly trustworthy. He was also stupid, like most of his ilk, stupid to spend money openly, stupid to lie, but there is a type of mania common to good-looking fresh-faced boys and men, often only sons, that leads them to believe they can get away with anything – and often, for a while, they do: as I recall it has something to do with the lack of any clear definition between right and wrong.

19. I rested my case with another drink which also helped to take my mind off the lingering headache I'd been having since Ben Hogan kindly cold-cocked me. I would have to think about him, too, some day soon, to say nothing of the amazing Mr Lubinski.

One thing at a time, I decided. I moved over to the Two-Two-Two but didn't linger as it was as deserted as the streets of Glasgow on Tag Day. So was Sandy's, maybe something truly momentous was going on that I didn't know about, like another invasion of the bodysnatchers or a Dallas rerun. Where was everybody? I called Evonne; she was out. I called Linda with the skinny legs, even she was out. So I went disconsolately home, remembering to keep an eye out for red-faced Micks who swung southpaw, like me.

I was up early the following morning as I wanted to have a word or two with Ricky before he went to work. I caught him on the way out, he told me. I told him some of the conclusions I'd come to the previous evening, and finished up by letting him know that his amigo Tommy didn't have a brother who got him deals on cars and shared expensive pads with him, all he had was a sister in New York and what did he think of that?

'I'm thinking what you're thinking,' Ricky said grimly. Then he swore a bit. 'I'll kill that maricón.'

'No you will not,' I said. 'At least not yet. We have to be very clever if we want to find out what really happened, so you be good. We'll get him, I promise, somehow, soon. Now listen. You do not tell Ellena anything for now, OK? She's got enough to worry about. Segundo. You've been to Tommy's house, tell me about it.'

'That fucker,' said Ricky. 'So what do you want to know, man? It's like a house.'

I told him what I wanted to know. Then he told me what I wanted to know, that there was a phone in the front hall just inside the door.

'Could be good,' I said. 'Ideally, what I want is for him to come from work tonight, pick up that phone and call his weed-growing friends up north.'

'You're gonna bug him, man?'

'I'm going to bug the shit out of him,' I said.

'But why that phone?'

'Because, Señor Watson, I can get to that phone without breaking into the house or posing as a telephone repairman or whatever, at least I think I can. Now, what you have to do is to give him an excellent reason to make him call his friends as soon as he gets home.'

'Like what?'

'Like this.' Mom put in an appearance then in an ancient dressing gown that had started out in life eons ago as a present from her to Pop. She waved good morning and went into the kitchen.

'Like this. You told me once that no one knew about Chico except you and Ellena, right?'

'Right. Except for Lucky, but he doesn't know who he is, just that he's a friend of mine.'

'But not Tommy?'

'Not Tommy.'

'Do you two get off work at the same time?'

'More or less, it all depends.'

'Well, make it happen today,' I said. 'That would be, what, about four thirty? Then, on your way out to your cars, you tell him you're worried. Come to think of it, you've been worried all day but you can't keep it to yourself anymore. You tell him about Chico, the cabin, the sheep, your visits to him, and now he's missing. You didn't know what to do so you asked me, the brilliant sleuth who solved the mystery of the missing mutton so quickly, to look into it. This, we hope, will put the fear of God into your amigo Tommy. He probably knows by now his buddies knocked off some guy who was sneaking around, but when said guy turns out to be your brother-in-law, he'll know he's got trouble, trouble right there in Parson's Crossing. Got it?'

'Yeah, I got it OK,' Ricky said. Then he said something in Spanish to his wife about not worrying, he knew what time it was and he wasn't going to be late.

'We've got to figure that Tommy will get on to his pals pronto and tell them to cool it for a while, close down, lay low, just in case I'm not as dumb as I look. If he starts heading back to the office to call from there, which is unlikely as the call would have to be put through by Mae's husband at the front desk, you tag along on some pretext, you've got more to tell him, whatever, so he'll have to give up that idea. Then, unfortunately, your car won't start as you have earlier done something clever to it, like graphite-ing the plugs to make sure it won't. Of course your buddy will have to give you a lift back into town. Got it?'

'I'm with you,' Ricky said. 'We don't want him to get to a phone til he gets home.'

'You do have it,' I said. Mom brought me in a cup of coffee and put it down on the table in front of me. 'Of course he can always stop after he drops you off and call from a bar or a payphone somewhere but it's more natural for a guy who's had the kind of shock Tommy's going to get to run for home first and then call, it's easier and more private and he doesn't need a pocketful of change. Anyway, it's worth a try and it doesn't cost us anything significant. If it doesn't work I can always get a read-out of his phone bill and see if he's been calling anyone regularly up north, in fact I'm going to do that anyway, but if his pals always call him instead of the other way round it wouldn't help us much.'

I then had Ricky go through his part of the action; he had it down pat and was raring to go, so I let him. Margarita blew me a kiss over the phone.

'Thank you, little one,' I said.

I had a second cup of coffee with Mom, who was not at her best that morning although she didn't say anything, drove to the office, where there was nothing in the mail to detain me, let alone make me rich, then took the Ventura Freeway east to Glendale. I parked in front of the retail outlet of J & M Home Security Co., which was tucked into a little side street off Brand right next to a struggling magic and joke store. I took a quick peek into the joke store's water-streaked window – same brilliant products I'd loved as a boy – fake ca ca, flies in ice cubes, soap that made you dirty instead of clean, disappearing ink, fake sick, X-ray specs. I once got a finger-guillotine trick in my Christmas stocking; my brother borrowed it and broke it.

I knew the chap behind the counter at J & M's as I'd done a fair bit of business with him over the years. Phil was his name, he looked like your typical space cadet – granny glasses, freaked-out hair, complexion riddled by youthful acne into something resembling a flour and water relief map of the Andes, T-shirt saying something dirty in Latin. But Phil knew his business and there was an extraordinary amount of business to know as almost daily more and more elaborate, miniaturized gimmicks entered the market.

He came up with a micro-transmitter the size of a dead pea, which is roughly what it looked like, or perhaps a tiny piece of gravel. With it came a small receiver, with headphones, much like a Walkman. The rig only had a range of some hundred yards but that would be more than enough. I had to buy the transmitter as it was unrecoverable and would hopefully end up unnoticed in Tommy's vacuum cleaner, but Phil let me rent the receiver for one day for $35 cash, no receipt.

I said, 'Phil, you're the tops in my book,' and left. I resisted the temptation to drop in next door and buy a new finger guillotine. There was one in the window, too, only in the illustration on the box they showed a cigarette instead of a finger so as not to give small boys ideas they had anyway.

On the way back I stopped at Moe's for a late breakfast of two hotdogs, mustard and relish only, and a root beer. A Mr Universe type next to me from the health club across the street was sipping a glass of hot water with a slice of lemon in it. I ordered a third hotdog from Son of Moe just to show him who was boss.

Back at the office. I had to make sure that Tommy had gone in to work that morning, as usual. I suspected that if he hadn't, Ricky would have called in to let me know, but just on the long shot that he'd tried me and I'd been out, I called the ranger station and Mae's husband told me both men were out on the job. Then I called the messenger service I used. I wanted a particular willing boy who had done a couple of errands for me in the past, but not knowing his name I had to describe him, which wasn't hard as he was young, good-looking and had shoulder-length blond hair. The girl who took the calls told me he was already out the door and heading my way and should she put it on the bill, as usual.

'Please do,' I said. While I waited for him I looked over the mail again. Will Mullins had sent me from the Hall downtown the material he'd promised me; I skimmed through some of it then put it all up on the bookshelf. I threw out all of the junk mail but one item, one of those teasers you get from real-estate companies promising you a valueless free gift if you'll only attend a weekend viewing of their latest tacky development project. I looked up Tommy's address in the phone book, typed it neatly on a clean envelope, and inserted the real-estate rubbish. About then my willing boy putt-putted up on his underpowered Yamaha, dismounted, took his helmet off, shook out his hair, knocked on my door and entered. He saluted me smartly.

'A task, willing boy,' I said to him. 'A well-paying task. Be seated and I will tell you all.'

'Nothing legal, I hope,' the kid said, sitting in the spare chair.

I looked shocked. 'Kids today,' I said sadly.

He grinned. He had perfect teeth. Everyone had perfect teeth but me. Except Son of Moe, he had terrible teeth, he sucked sugar cubes all day.

'So what is it this time, Chief?' the kid asked me. 'A spot of breaking and entering? A trail job?'

'A plain, ordinary special delivery,' I said, handing over the envelope. 'All you are required to do is deliver this harmless envelope to the address written on it. It is an address in Sherman Oaks. Sherman Oaks is west of here.'

'And,' said the kid. He took out a green plastic comb big enough to curry llamas and lovingly rearranged his locks.

'And,' I said, 'you drop this little bugger inside the letter slot at the same time, endeavoring to make it land as close to the wall as possible so it will not be noticed.' I handed him over the dried pea. 'Treat it carefully, my boy, it is a triumph of micro-circuitry.'

'Looks like a mouse turd to me,' said the kid, 'but I'll take your word for it. Oh, might one inquire about one's fee?'

We settled on a twenty for him in addition to the agency's standard charge. He unlimbered, got up, saluted again, and started for the door.

'Might one inquire what your name is?' I said to his back. 'I'm tired of having to describe you to what's-her-name who answers your phone.'

'My name is George,' the kid said. 'But all the girls call me Gorgeous.'

'Well, Gorgeous,' I said, 'do me a favor. Call in and tell me how it goes, maybe there isn't a letter slot in the door, maybe there's a tin thing beside the front gate, maybe there's a dog who won't let you in.'

'Will do, Chief,' he said.

I wrote the office number on a slip of paper and gave it to him. He tucked it in one glove and left. I phoned the one and only punk twerp, Sara Silvetti, world's worst poet by far.

She was in. She was busy. She was actually hard at work. Didn't I know that writing poetry was the hardest work there was?

'No I didn't,' I said. 'I was under the mistaken illusion that working in coal mines was harder, or growing bananas or extruding aluminum. Ever so sorry. Gee, I've always thought scribbling verses was fairly easy work, you sit at a desk in a nice warm room eating popcorn and once in a while sharpen a pencil or two.'

She sighed. 'Why do old farts always take so long to get to the point?'

I sighed. 'All right, Mrs Barrett Bloody Browning, how much do I love you, let me count the ways, none, you want a job? Maybe two jobs?'

'Doing what?'

'Get over here and find out, if you can possibly tear yourself away from that couplet that just won't quite somehow come out right.'

I hung up, set up the computer and did some work. Twenty minutes later she walked in without knocking and it hurt just to look at her. When last I'd seen her, her hair had been a wiry mop one third a modest day-glo orange, one third a discreet Day-Glow lime green, and the remaining third a restful electric blue. Now it was all shaven off except for a round patch on top that was tinted pink, it made her look like she was about to clean the bottom of a large pot. She had a black spiderweb either drawn or tattooed on one cheek and a large tear painted on the other. I won't bother describing her clothes in any detail, as who would be interested, but suffice it to say that it was the first time I'd ever seen a feather boa, a tatty fur piece and a man's old-fashioned Celluloid stiff collar around the same skinny neck. I might perhaps mention her footwear, huge cowboy boots with spurs.

'Greetings, Gramps,' she said. 'How're they hangin'?'

'None of your business,' I said. 'Can you still borrow that car that belongs to that friend of yours?'

'Nah,' she said. 'His father finally lowered the boom on him. I can get another one, though. Jerry's not doin' nothin', he's got a car.'

'A proper car that won't be noticed, I hope,' I said, 'not some dune buggy or low-rider special.'

'It's a car,' she said. 'What else can I tell you?'

'Can you get it today?'

'No sweat, Pops,' she said. She produced a panatella from somewhere and a box of kitchen matches from somewhere else and lit up with a lot of unnecessary dramatics.

I told her what to do and when to do it and how much she would get if she did do it. I showed her how to work the receiver and handed it over. I told her to keep Saturday morning free because I might have another job for her then if she didn't muck up the first one.

'Knowing how cheap you are,' she said, blowing smoke in my direction, 'how's about a fin for expenses in advance?'

I gave her the money, anything to get that cigar out of my office and her with it. Me, cheap? Hadn't I given a generous handout to that panhandler in front of Ralph's a mere two or three days earlier?

CHAPTER ELEVEN

My nose hurt. I went into the small bathroom at the back and looked at it in the pitted mirror over the sink. It looked like a nose with dirty adhesive tape on it. It made me think about Mr G. so I thought I'd have a try at finding him if it didn't take too long, if my wits were up to the struggle.

Let us see. I knew the missus was Catholic and worked at it, thus she probably attended church regularly if not five times a day. I suspected she was local as she had come to me rather than someone else in another part of town, and not in a car. Also, when I'd seen her on the bench at the bus stop across from me she hadn't caught the 202 bus that stopped there and it was the only line that ran down Victory, and it had been half empty. Maybe she was just sitting there thinking things over and planned to catch the next one but it was also possible she wasn't waiting for a bus at all as she lived so close she didn't need one.

There were two churches within a four-block distance of my office, the phone book informed me, Christ the King and Our Lady of All Sorrows. I thought Mrs Morales might know something about them as I knew she was a Catholic because the only day in the year she closed was on her Saint's Day, and I also knew she lived locally as once I'd driven her daughter home after work. I was on my way out to talk with her when the phone called me back. It was Gorgeous reporting in as requested.

'No problem, Chief,' he said. 'Piece of cake. I lobbed her against the wall like I was shootin' marbles.'

'Good work, my boy,' I said. I told him I'd include his twenty in a separate envelope when I paid the monthly bill from the messenger service, hung up, and dropped by Taco-Burger. It was just on noon, a little early for lunch, but a growing boy can always eat a taco or two, even Mrs Morales'. After a certain amount of obligatory badinage with her I asked her about Christ the King and Our Lady of All Sorrows.

'I wouldn't be seen dead in Our Lady,' she said angrily, unscrewing the top of a bottle of cream soda for me. 'That Father, he only likes white people, comprende?'

I said I comprendo-ed.

'Now our Father Xavier, he don't look like much but he comes, day or night, rain or snow, money or not. What you want with him? You not suddenly getting religion at your age?'

'More than that, Juanita,' I told her soberly. 'I've decided to sell out and become a monk. I wonder what summers in Tibet are like?'

'Oh, you,' Mrs Morales said, giving my hand a playful slap.

'Enough of that,' I said. 'And where's the hot salsa today?'

Christ the King was close enough so that I didn't need the car; I locked up then ambled down Victory – past Lubinski, Lubinski and Levi, as it happened – then made a left, then a right, and there it was. It didn't look much like a church to me, being a rather arty combination of brick, redwood and concrete, but what do I know about churches, especially contemporary Catholic ones. It did however have a cross, a very large one, replacing the traditional steeple.

The front door was open, so I went in. The inside looked marginally more traditional, if you discount the deep rose wall-to-wall carpeting, and after all this was California. There were several of what I took to be confessional booths on either side of the entrance at the back, then the rows of empty pews, with a large statue on either side of the lectern up front. I couldn't see any officials or priests or nuns or cardinals or popes about so I took a seat at the back and tried to remember the last time I'd been in a Catholic church. It would have been at least five years ago out in Venice for the funeral of a friend of me and my brother, actually one of his best friends, old Ed, who had been his mentor, or rabbi, as they say, when he first joined the police. Old Ed had killed himself one Sunday afternoon about three months after his retirement, in his kitchen, but the department let out that it had been accidental to try and make it easier for the widow, to avoid any problems with his pension or insurance and to make it possible for him to have a proper Catholic burial in consecrated ground. Then I thought about Mr Lubinski and gold, then I ran out of things to think about so I just sat there looking down at my big feet.

Finally a priest came into the church from a door up behind the lectern I hadn't noticed and after genuflecting he made his way down the center aisle toward me. I followed him out into the vestibule and found him thumbtacking a piece of paper up on the noticeboard beside the door. When I got closer I saw it was headed 'Sport's news from the All-Catholic Basketball League'.

'Excuse me,' I said, keeping my voice low. 'Have you a minute?'

'I do indeed,' he said loudly, holding out a hand. 'I'm Father Sean.'

'Victor Daniel,' I said. He shook my hand vigorously. He was a young man with a pale, freckled face, in full uniform complete with dog-collar.

'Pardon my ignorance, Father,' I said, 'but are you in charge here?'

'I am not,' he said. 'That would be Father O'Keefe but he's away for the day.'

'Ah,' I said. 'I suppose he's a very busy man.'

'He is indeed,' said the Father with a straight face. 'His golfing duties alone take up three afternoons a week.'

I laughed; we moved more or less by common consent out on to the wide front steps. He looked up at the cloudy January sky, sighed with pleasure, at what I couldn't figure out, then asked me how he could be of help.

I asked him if he knew most of his parishioners. He told me he knew most of the regular churchgoers, certainly. I then told him of my visit from Mrs 'Gillespie' and that I was worried about her and wanted to see her again and as I suspected she was both local and a regular worshipper, wondered if he could help me locate her. When I described her and her recent injuries, he said, 'Oh, dear God, that poor woman. Yes of course I know her. I've talked to her many times and so has Father O'Keefe and it's to our great sorrow we've not been able to help her.'

'Well, maybe I can,' I said.

He gave me a long look.

'Maybe I'm not bound by quite the same restrictions you are,' I said.

'I very much doubt that you are,' he said. He turned and looked up at the front of his church. 'Is beauty entirely in the eye of the beholder?'

I told him I'd never thought about it much.

He turned back to me. 'Mr Daniel, we are obliged to follow, strictly follow, the Catholic pronunciamento on divorce, which is roughly that we are against it in almost all circumstances even if one of the parties involved is from time to time being physically abused by the other party. The wisdom of such a stipulation and the anomalies it often produces are constantly being debated by the appropriate church authorities as well as by us lesser mortals, as obviously no one likes to see needless suffering. However, we are bound to live by church law and to live within it. I would hate to admit publicly that there are times when prayer and faith and charity and love of God and respect for fellow human beings are not enough, but I am also not blind. Perhaps you can do something for her that we can't. Her name is Mary Bridget

Donovan, her husband's name is Kevin. They have no children and they live in an apartment building called the Palmettos on Belvedere Drive. I've been there several times but I don't recall the apartment number.'

'Thank you,' I said. We shook hands again.

'God be with you,' he said, and headed briskly back into his church. I headed slowly out to the street and retraced my steps back to Lubinski, Lubinski and Levi, family jewelers for over twenty years. On the way I saw a small brown dog get run over and killed by a large black limo which didn't stop, which was just as well for the driver given how I feel about dogs. And limos. By the time I got to the dog it was already dead. I borrowed a newspaper from a horrified middle-aged lady who bravely accompanied me out into the traffic, wrapped up the poor unidentifiable mutt in it and laid it to rest in a garbage can in front of Arrow Liquors.

'Poor thing,' said the lady.

I could only nod in agreement.

At the jeweler's. The front picture window was crisscrossed by a protective iron grid. The reinforced glass front door was locked; a small sign said 'Ring for entrance'. I did. My client peeped out, saw it was only harmless old me and let me in. I deduced immediately that he was glad to see me because he seized one of my hands in both of his, pressed it warmly, and said, 'Am I glad to see you.' He looked nervously over his shoulder at a man I presumed was his cousin Nate Lubinski, a tall, lugubrious individual who was at the back of the store talking to a customer, then he whispered to me, 'So what's the plan?'

'Can we talk here?' I whispered back.

'Why not?' he said in a more normal voice. 'Just so we shouldn't shout at the top of our lungs. You want to see something from the window, right? So we go to the window.'

So we went to the window and looked for a moment at his window display.

'Schlock for the tourists,' Mr Lubinski said, looking fondly down at his own gold tiepin and adjusting it slightly.

'Tomorrow,' I said. 'When your Italian friend comes, we are going to take his picture and we are also going to get his fingerprints.'

'We are also going to die,' said Mr Lubinski in alarm, 'And as my wife said to me just the other day, I'm too old to die. You think that crook, that mobster is going to smile for the birdie while I take some candid snaps of him for my album? You're looking at a dead man.'

'You are not going to take his picture,' I said. 'My assistant, who will be cleverly disguised as a punk rocker, will take his picture without him knowing a thing about it.'

'A punk?' Mr Lubinski's eyebrows almost disappeared under his hairline. 'What do they know from pictures? What do they know from anything except how to disappoint their hardworking parents?' He waved at a lady who passed in front of the shop. 'Mrs Margolin. She still owes me for her daughter's graduation ring. Twenty-four carat, with the initials in diamond chips.'

'What's the difference between twenty-four carat and, say, eighteen?' I asked him.

'Some copper, a pinch of nickel, and a lot of money,' he said. 'Most jewelry is eighteen because it's the easiest to work.'

'Oh,' I said.

'Oh,' he repeated. 'So what about the fingerprints, who's going to take them from that killer, some other assistant, a Hell's Angel biker maybe?'

'You,' I said.

'I'm a dead man again,' he said. He saw his cousin's client making her way to the front door and politely opened it for her. When she had left, he called back to his partner, 'So what was that, Mr Lubinski?'

'The pearl three-strand, Mr Lubinski,' Cousin Nate called back. Both Mr Lubinskis looked pleased.

'All you do,' I told my Mr Lubinski, 'is show him some gold. You said he wears a lot, right? So you show him some, in a box, in a box you have wiped clean first. And not a velvet box, either, or one with ridges all over it, a plain, smooth box. You say, "With respect, sir, I see you are a lover of fine gold. That chain around your neck is particularly fine. Please have a quick look at this." And you offer him the box, holding it carefully by one end. What is he going to do?'

'Kill me,' said Mr Lubinski gloomily. 'With his bare hands. Or maybe strangle me with his particularly fine chain, which by the way was a piece of junk.'

'No he won't,' I said patiently. 'You have already disarmed him by telling him as you seem to have no choice and as you're after all a sensible man with a loving wife, you will take his gold, at his price, whenever he says.'

'If I do that, I'm dead again,' said Mr Lubinski, 'only differently. Then what, though believe me I hate to ask?'

'Then,' I said, 'you pack your bags and prepare to head east because if, as I suspect, your Italian turns out really to have serious connections, I'd be happier if you were out of town for a while.'

'You'd be happier,' said Mr Lubinski, rolling his eyes. 'That's a good one. And what do I tell my wife, you're so smart? Say, "Listen, darling, it's just a whim but I suddenly realized I've never seen Philadelphia in January"?'

'What about the truth?'

'What? After thirty-two years of marriage? Then she'd really think something was wrong.'

I grinned at him.

'So when are we talking about, all this?' he asked.

'Probably tomorrow night,' I said. 'I'll give you a call. I also think you should put all your good pieces in a bank vault somewhere, make sure your insurance is paid up, and also close up for a couple of weeks, no sense risking anyone else getting hurt.'

'Mr Lubinski!' he called out immediately. 'Take two weeks off starting Monday!'

'Why's that?' Mr Lubinski called back.

'We're closing up! I'm going to Switzerland for a nose job, if anyone asks.' He said to me, 'Speaking of noses, how's yours coming along?'

I told him it was tender but coming along fine, my doctor said I'd look just like John Garfield after the swelling went down.

'A good Jewish boy,' Mr Lubinski said approvingly, letting me out. 'So what time does your punk get here tomorrow?'

'Early,' I said. 'Be nice to her, her feelings are easily hurt.'

'A lady punk?' he said. 'In Lubinski, Lubinski and Levi? Mr Lubinski! Your two weeks, they start tomorrow, not Monday!'

What next? Wade's, maybe, for some kind of camera that could take close-ups of Italian mobsters without getting the photographer annihilated. I strolled back to the office, picked up the car and drove east out to Wade's garage, on Domingo, near the turn-off for the Burbank Airport. It was really Wade's brother and sister-in-law's garage but the kid requisitioned it when he set up in business on his own providing a photo developing service. For once Wade wasn't dozing in the Mexican hammock he'd strung up beside the garage, he was actually in the garage working. His new labrador puppy Shusha was in the hammock instead. I rapped on the door and after a moment it opened a couple of inches and Wade's thin, white, goateed face peered out. It didn't brighten noticeably when he saw who it was.

'Oh,' he said. 'You.'

'Me,' I said. 'You were expecting maybe Karsh of Ottawa?'

'Want some coffee?' he said.

'Always,' I said. We traipsed up the path to the kitchen and went in. A cat that had been waiting patiently on the porch came in with us. While Wade heated up the large enamel coffee pot that was on the stove and gave the cat a handful of some dry munchies, I told him what I needed.

'Can do,' he said.

'By the way, why do you keep that Goddamned scary thing in here?' I asked him. I was referring to an enormous tarantula in a large, enclosed glass case which was hung on the wall right over the kitchen table.

'You mean Maria?' he said. ''Cause it's the warmest room in the house is why.'

'Well, why do you keep the Goddamn thing at all?'

'Don't ask me, man,' he said, pouring out the coffee. 'It's Cissy's. Ask her. I only feed it once in a while when she's away.'

'I won't ask you what on,' I said. We took our coffees back to the garage, the cat following us. Wade took a camera case down from a shelf and passed it to me.

'What's this?' he asked me.

I opened up the case and took out a camera about the size of a Leica.

'It's a camera,' I said.

'What does it do?'

'It probably takes pictures,' I said. 'As you know, I have a camera, a Canon, and it takes pictures too.'

'Ah, but what kind of pictures does this one take?' He stroked his wispy beard with inner amusement.

'Give me a break, Wade,' I said. 'I don't have all day, some of us do have work to do.' I took a closer look at the camera.

'Ah ha,' I said. 'Does this one take pictures around corners?'

'It sure do,' he said. 'At right angles, to be precise.' He showed me how it worked; there wasn't much to it. Due to either a mirror or a prism, when you looked through the viewfinder what you actually saw through a second, concealed lens, was the area directly to your left.

'They were quite the thing at one time,' he told me smugly. 'Henri Cartier-Bresson and all that, the decisive moment, take your shot when they're not looking and get out alive. They still make them. I took this in a trade last year.'

'Can I borrow it for a day?'

'Help yourself,' he said. He rummaged around in a drawer that was next to his color developer, came up with a roll of film, loaded it and wound it in in half the time it would have taken me. 'Voilà.'

While I was thanking him, a timer went off which meant he had work to do so I left him to it and drove back to my part of town. I wasn't completely sure if that lamebrain Sara could learn to operate the camera but I had no one else to use. I looked too much like muscle, Willing Boy was a possibility if he could get the time off but he came expensive, the chiseler, and my pal and occasional accomplice Benny wouldn't get up that early on a Saturday morning for a date with Bo Derek on a topless beach.

On the way back home I detoured slightly and parked about a half a block down from the Palmettos where the Donovans lived, just to see what I could see. I gave it a good hour with a break or two to stretch my aching legs, but there was no sign of either one of them.

To hell with it. I had to move Mom over to my brother's so the big showdown with Mr Kevin Lefty Donovan would have to wait. But bloody revenge is that much sweeter when it is postponed, someone said once. I think it was Albert Schweitzer but I'm not positive.

CHAPTER TWELVE

My mother was in her room taking a nap. I couldn't see any signs of packing so I presumed she'd forgotten it was moving day.

I had an agreement with my brother Tony and his wife Gaye which worked pretty well. We each had Mom for three weeks in turn. It was probably hardest on Gaye, Mom didn't like her or, I suspected, think she was good enough for her favorite, her youngest, her special boy Tony. If anything, I thought she was too good for him. But Mom got on well with their two kids, Martine, ten, and Martin, eleven already, and they seemed to like having their old Gran around to spoil them. I tried to keep my mouth shut about the part of the arrangement I didn't like at all, being a true Easterner, which was having to live somewhere reasonably near both Tony and Mom's doctor, i.e., in the land that God either forgot or never knew about in the first place, the San Fernando Valley. Big deal. 'I cried for louder music and I called for stronger wine,' my long-gone pop used to shout to amuse his boys. Or something like that.

When Mom woke up we got her packed, with the usual problems of what to take and what to wear and this and that. She said goodbye to her crony Feeb downstairs who told me, as she always did, to drive extra special as I only had one mom. That I already knew.

So I dropped her off; Tony wasn't home yet but Gaye and the kids were there to settle her in. I kissed her goodbye like she liked me to do and then the kids took her out back to the garden to show her something totally fab and non-gross, I never did find out what it was. Then Gaye politely offered me a drink, as she always did, and I politely took a rain check, as I always did. I suppose that summed up our relationship, a sort of forced politeness. We had no chemistry at all going. I wasn't sure how much she had left with my brother but that was none of my business, thank God, as I had plenty of other things to worry about that were my business, one of which being how Ricky and Sara had fared. They were both supposed to phone in and let me know so I went back to the office to wait for their calls. I thought about setting up Betsy and doing something constructive but I wound up looking at the wall and musing instead. When the phone finally did ring, it was Evonne asking me for a date.

'Gee, you've got a nerve,' I said, 'calling a popular guy at the last minute like this.'

'Can it,' she said. 'Pick you up in an hour?'

'Oh no,' I said. 'I'll pick you up in an hour. I may be a little late, I'm waiting on a couple of calls. Where are you taking me, dearest, not to the theater again I hope?'

'A party,' she said, 'one of the teachers is retiring. Wish I was.'

'I may not have time to go home and change,' I said.

'With you there's not a lot of difference,' she said. 'See you.' She hung up; I went back to my musing. I mused about blonds who had a strange, illicit passion for summer squashes and wore cherry and raspberry-flavored lipstick and drove like they were blindfolded. Then I looked up my stars in the *Herald Examiner* – romance beckons, but examine your motives, it said. For once they were dead right.

It was five thirty when Ricky phoned in; he was in a hurry due to some domestic crisis and only had time to tell me all had gone as planned at his end. Sara phoned an hour later.

'Confidential agent X-2 reporting in by telephone from corner of Tangerine and Wilcox,' she said. 'All clear your end?'

'Get on with it,' I said. 'You really are the limit.'

'Mission accomplished,' she whispered. 'Full detailed report will be delivered to you by hand before midnight. Out.'

'Wait a minute, wait a minute. Why don't you deliver your full, detailed report by hand tomorrow morning instead, at, say, eight fifteen, if you can get up that early.'

'Dying to see me in ze flesh, eh, Boss?' she said. 'Startin' to get to you am I?'

'You must be kidding, Junior,' I said. 'I got another task for you, near here, and you have to be there by nine. You'll like this mission, you stand an excellent chance of getting torn apart in very small pieces by a very large Italian who loathes punks.'

'Thanks ever so, Gramps,' she said. 'See you in the morning then and try not to have a hangover, you're miserable enough anyway.' She hung up on me, the obnoxious twerp. Was she lucky she'd run into someone as tolerant and easygoing as me, no one else in their right or even wrong mind would put up with her.

However. I picked up Evonne and off we went to the party. I wasn't expecting much, teachers being what they are, but was I wrong. When we got there the joint was already jumping and it was still jumping when we left just before two and for all I know it continues to jump to this day. Someone emptied a family-size box of Duz in the Jacuzzi with the usual spectacular results. Two middle-aged lady teachers who were stripped down to their stretch marks started a dart game in the garage using a spear gun instead of darts. When we finally reluctantly did leave, the third re-run of *Deep Throat* was showing on the TV in the master bedroom. I drove extra carefully, partly to show Evonne by example what good driving was, in the one in a million chance that some of it might rub off on her, but also because, I must admit, I'd had a few. Evonne snuggled up beside me, smelling deliciously of all those wondrous things gorgeous women smell of — shampoo and perfume and nailpolish and tobacco and lipstick and bourbon and skin.

When we got to her place and I'd walked her to the back door, she asked me casually if I wanted to come in for a minute. I examined my motives carefully before I said yes, please.

And came the morn, if I may wax poetic one time only. And came the morn and came a very happy boy whistling his way homeward, whistling his way up the steps of his apartment, whistling in the shower, attempting to whistle while drinking his morning java, etc.

I made it to the office right on time and was just opening up when I saw Sara get off the bus across the street. Then I stopped whistling. She crossed the street against the lights, made a rude gesture at a motorist who had to brake sharply to avoid her, stopped on the sidewalk to gaze up at great length at the cloudy sky in what she obviously hoped was a forlornly poetic manner but was really only obvious, then she deigned to enter my office, the door to which I had been patiently holding open for her for some considerable time.

'Nice outfit,' I told her, heading briskly for the chair on my side of the desk before she got to it. 'I've always liked the look of calico on the slimmer figure.'

'Fuck off,' she said. She dug a sheaf of papers out of her reticule, or whatever foolishness it was. 'Here. Read and inwardly digest, Pops.'

'You need a new ribbon,' I said. 'Make that a new typewriter.' Then I read:

CONFIDENTIAL

16 Jan.
Report.
From: Agent S.S.

To: V.D. (Ha ha)
   (From notes taken in the field)
As per instructions
Arrived at stake-out
11311 Williams Boulevard, Sherman Oaks,
San Fernando Valley, California, USA, North America, Western Hemisphere, Earth, Milky Way, Universe
at five pee em Friday 16 Jan. 1985,
Accompanied by Jerry G. (address on request) in his 68 Ford dragster.
For disguise purposes we both had large Cokes.
I paid: Expenses: $1.40
Checked the time from the car radio.
Tested receiver, got only static.
Jerry G., who is almost cute in an icky surfer way
Tested his Walkman. Together we looked like your typical teenagers
Of today, each listening intently to his own deafening interior music.
Sipped Cokes. Man in shorts across street began watering his lawn.
Dog from next door snuck through hedge. Man pretended to ignore dog.
Dog pretended to ignore man. Man suddenly turned and tried to spray
Dog who jumped just out of reach. End of animal act.
A housewife or two drove up and into driveways and began unloading
Suburban survival kits – booze, charcoal an' sour cream dips.
5.42. Suspect arrives in Toyota hatchback, smokin' rubber.
Hops out, opens garage (not locked) runs car in. Heads for his front
Door.
I switch on receiver ... AND HEAR HIM GO IN!!

AND HEAR HIM GO STRAIGHT TO PHONE.
  AND HEAR THIS:

(Written down by me AS IT HAPPENED)

(Faint sounds of someone pushing push-button phone)

Dell there, please? (Pause)

Dell? It's me. Your stupid fucking asshole brother there too?

(From now on, pauses indicated by '. . .')

. . . Oh, no? Well have I got news for him, that wasn't just
  some

Fucking tramp wetback he creamed, he was only the fucking
  brother-

In-law of the fucking guy I work with, Ricky, how does that
  grab ya? . . .

Because he told me, that's how I know, he's been hiding him
  out

In the Goddamned woods for years . . . because he was nuts,
  that's why,

Not completely nuts, but nuts enough . . . you're telling me
  . . .

Oh, another little thing you might like to tell your baby
  brother,

Ricky hired a detective to look around . . . some huge, fat
  jerk, I

Met him, a nothing . . . yeah, I think so too, don't go near the
  place,

Why take any chances, leave it, fuck it for a couple of weeks
  . . .

If we keep cool, not a chance . . . I can always find out
  from my good

Buddy Rick, can't I, exactly when he gets tired of paying off
  that

Big jerkoff who's not getting nowhere and tells him to fuck
  off . . .

OK . . . OK . . . Yeah. You better believe it.

Phone call terminated at 5.46.

Waited a few moments in case he phoned anyone else.
Negative.
Stake-out concluded at 5.51.
Stop for gas at Arco:
I paid: Expenses: $4.00
Then gave Jerry the brush-off.
Phoned you from home, line busy.
Phoned again and reported.
Mom says hello.
I says goodbye.
You owe me forty cents (see 'Expenses')
PAY UP OR ELSE
S.S.

Total expenses: $5.40
From . . . $5.00
You owe me   .40

'Here,' I said. I tossed a quarter, a dime and a nickel on the desk.

'What about my wages, you quote big jerkoff unquote?'

'What about my receiver, you money-grubber?'

She dug it out of her carry-all and handed it over.

'I figure you owe me plenty because first of all it could have been dangerous and second of all it wasn't exactly legal.'

'Oh, come on.' I said wearily. 'If I did give you a lot of money you'd only spend it on hash brownies or a Madonna wig. Here.' I dug out ten bucks with pretended reluctance. 'And sign here.' I took out a pad of receipt forms from the left-hand top drawer, making sure she didn't see the .38 that was also in there, and had her sign on the dotted line.

'What a cheapskate,' she said. 'It's unbelievable, really.'

'You're lucky to get anything,' I said. 'Most apprentices work the first five years for nothing. Now if you're done complaining, let me tell you about your next little caper.'

I told her. I showed her how to work the camera that took

pictures at right angles. I assured her that I had been there and there was plenty of natural light. I suggested that her cover might be that of a student who was doing a series on local businessmen for a school assignment for a journalism course. I suggested she buy a large notebook to scribble in. I suggested she snap pictures like crazy all over the place, like they always seem to do, and be more or less finishing up when the Italian came. 'Be studentlike,' I told her, 'despite your appearance.'

'How do you know what students are like today, Pops?' she said, ruffling her bizarre haircut with one gloved hand. 'Living in the eighteenth century like you do.' Maybe she did have a point. I had been wrong about teachers.

'Be nice to Mr Lubinski,' I said. 'You'll like him. Maybe you could be the daughter he never had.'

'Ha ha,' she said. 'What's he like?'

'Hysterical,' I said, 'as you will see if you ever get off your bony butt.'

'What's the Italian like?' she said, not moving.

'Trouble, a lot of trouble,' I said. 'So be careful, if anything goes wrong, you split. If you think you can't handle it when the time comes, you split. Got it?'

'Whoooo,' she said, moving at last. 'Who's getting soft in his old age?'

'Are you kidding?' I laughed. 'I've got a fortune invested in that camera, that's all.'

'That's more like the Pops I know,' she said. She grinned at me for some reason and left, leaving the door open behind her in a childish attempt to irritate me. What a hope.

A short while after she left I began to get a bit restless. It was too early for the mail and I had nothing really that had to be done so I thought I'd take myself for a healthy walk. My left thigh was still tight, maybe some exercise would help. You know you're getting old when there's always at least one part of your body that hurts. I gingerly unpeeled the tape from my nose first; it didn't look too bad but it didn't look too good, either, in fact it had never looked that good after the first time I broke it, or rather, someone broke it for me.

By mere chance, some few minutes later I found myself almost directly across the street from Lubinski, Lubinski and Levi, in Mrs Martel's stationery shop, to be precise. After exchanging pleasantries with her, I popped into the post office next door to buy some stamps I didn't need, then I looked at the posters of people who were wanted for post office fraud, from where I could see through the window to the jeweler's across the way. I couldn't see any movement inside. Then I had a tiny, expensive glass of fresh orange juice at a health-food bar a couple of stores up the line.

Just on ten o'clock I saw what had to be our man. He got out of a passing Buick, waved nonchalantly to the driver, who took off, took one look around, then went up to Lubinski's and pressed the doorbell. Mr Lubinski let him in and closed the door behind him. I had decided to try and move closer, perhaps to amble casually past the store for a quick peek, but I'd no sooner hit the street when Mr Lubinski let Sara out. I ducked back into the health-food rip-off bar before she spotted me, I didn't want her to get any silly ideas that I was worried about her or couldn't trust her to do a simple job on her own. She said something with great animation to Mr Lubinski and then, instead of getting the hell out of there, posed him with painstaking care in front of his window and pretended to take his bloody picture. One hundred percent nerd.

By walking briskly, I managed to make it back to the office before she got there. In fact when she came hurrying in I'd dug out a piece of junk mail from the wastepaper basket, something that was offering me a chance to buy a lot of magazines I didn't want, and I was studying it with deep concentration.

'I got it!' she said. 'I got him cold!'

'Uh-huh,' I said. 'I wonder whether Mommy would rather have two years of *Good Housekeeping* or one year of *Sports Illustrated*.'

'I got it, sucker!' Sara said, ruffling my carefully arranged hair.

'Don't do that,' I said.

'I got the mother's prints too, looky here.' She took a small jewelry box out of her bag, with great care, holding it by the end. I put down, with a sigh, the literature I was pretending to peruse.

'How did you get that?'

'I can give no details at this time,' she said snootily, bouncing around the room. 'It will all be in my report, as usual. And that camera is a gas, man, would I like one of those.'

'Give,' I said. She dug it out and handed it over.

'Well?' she said then.

'Well what?'

'Aren't you gonna say, well done me old mate, or something like that?'

'Yes, I am, just this once,' I said, looking her right in her skinny puss. 'Well done me old mate.' And I gave her hair or coif or whatever it was a ruffle of its own.

'Don't overdo it,' she said, but she looked pleased all the same. 'When do you need the report by?'

I didn't really need another of her free-verse reports ever but I told her I had to have it by that afternoon at the latest. The rest of the case might depend on it.

'You got it, Pops,' she said, and off she went at a trot, presumably to start burning up her cheap typewriter.

What the hell. Maybe I was getting soft in my old age. Soft in the head.

CHAPTER THIRTEEN

There are one or two advantages in working for the Los Angeles Police Department, as my brother Tony found out. The pension plan is generous and old ladies and small children up to the age of six look up to you, except in brown or black barrios where children stop looking up to you as soon as their eyes open. There are also several disadvantages, as Tony's wife Gaye found out, little niggles like all policemen are hated until they're needed, their high divorce rate, their even higher rate of alcoholism and of course the good chance of getting highly injured as they go about their normal day's work.

One of the lesser-known advantages, if that's the right word, is that you are issued a personal code number and with that as identification you can call a certain department of Pacific Bell and they will give you without a hassle otherwise classified information – two unlisted numbers at a time or perhaps a list of a suspect's (or wife's) phone calls for any given period.

I had a call I wanted traced – the one Tommy DeMarco made to Dell on Friday afternoon, and if it was a long-distance one, even one of those short long-distance ones that they bill you an extra twelve cents for, there would be a record of it.

So I phoned the appropriate department, gave Tony's code, which I had memorized one time when he carelessly left it lying around in the top drawer of the desk in his den, stated my modest needs to the lady on the other end of the line, looked out the window for a minute, then was told that at 5.43 on 16 January one DeMarco, Thomas, L., had phoned one Tim's Tavern, in Carmen Springs, California.

'Where in hell's that?' I asked the lady.

'I don't know but it's twenty-six cents a minute away,' she said. 'Hang on, I'll ask my supervisor, according to her she knows everything.'

I hung on. I looked out the window again. It needed a clean but there was no more Timmy coming by a couple of times a week to do it for me. What did come by were two high-school kids on their way to Taco-Burger. When they saw the sign on my door, they laughed and waggled their fingers suggestively at me. Probably doper friends of Sara. Finally the lady came back.

'We think it's this side of Mojave somewhere,' she said.

'Thank you very much,' I said, 'that helps,' although it didn't really. I already knew approximately where Carmen Springs had to be, somewhere not too far away from the northern boundary of the forestry land. Ricky had official 1:1000 surveyors' maps, of course, I'd seen them, or one of them, on his desk, but I didn't want to talk to him over the phone if he was at work, and if he was at home he wouldn't have the maps. That made sense, I thought. I tried looking it up in the atlas I had on the shelf which I'd bought from a second-hand bookstore one time but either Carmen Springs was too small or it hadn't been invented yet when my fifteen-year-old atlas was printed, like most of California. Garages had maps. Mrs Martel had maps and she was on my visiting list for the day, but that wasn't til later so I left it for the while.

First stop though was Wade. I slung the camera round my neck, slipped the jewelry box carefully into a clean envelope, got the receiver from the safe, hit the road and was soon chugging through bustling, downtown Burbank toward Wade's place of business.

He was not in his hammock or the garage or the kitchen. His sister-in-law Cissy told me he was still in bed with Suze.

'Go get 'em up,' she said. She was trickling some pellets

into a cage of white mice. I didn't ask who the mice were for, if not for Maria the tarantula, who?

When I walked into Wade's bedroom he took one look at me, then hid under the covers, taking with him the breakfast joint he was smoking. .

'Go away,' he said, his voice muffled. 'Far, far away. Send him away, Suze. He's trouble. Get rid of him. Scare him. Show him your tattoo.'

Wade's girfriend, a short black girl with bow legs and the biggest grin this side of heaven where dwells Louis Armstrong, blazed her smile at me and giggled. After a minute, when Wade came up for air, I gave him back his camera and talked him into printing up right away a proof sheet of the one roll Sarah had shot by the simple manoeuvre of offering him double his normal stiff price.

'Any of a man, large, young, Italian, gold chain, white sports coat, Panama, give me three by fives too, O K?'

'I guess so,' said Wade, slowly getting out of bed. 'Up, you,' he said to Suze. 'When Wade's up, no one sleeps.'

While he was working, I put down three poached eggs and a stack of white toast with honey at that greasy spoon around the corner from him where the coffee was easily as bad as Mae's and weaker, too. What's the matter with you, America? You can make excellent hotdogs, delicious buttermilk pancakes and great ribs, what's so hard about coffee? Remind me to write a slim monograph about coffee sometime.

It was a strange collection of snaps I got back from Wade about half an hour later, some were of nothing, some were of parts of heads, one was of the twerp herself, taken at arm's length, in which she was grinning idiotically, but there were two of our Italian friend, one in particular a beauty as it showed him with Mr Lubinski. Score one for Sara.

I made the appropriate expressions of deep gratitude, kissed Suze on her warm, chocolate cheek, found the eastbound freeway, took one of the Glendale exits, parked in an official parking lot, and walked over to J & M Home Security Co. I made appropriate expressions of gratitude as I gave Phil back the receiver, then I gave him my shopping list for the day. He looked at it, nodding several times.

'You rentin' or buying?'

'Renting what I can rent, buying what I have to buy.'

I wound up buying another micro-transmitter, which Phil referred to as a transponder, larger than the one that looked like a dried pea, with a range of a couple of miles, in a waterproof rubber sheath. I rented the Geiger counter-like receiving set that went with it. It differed from a Geiger counter in that it didn't give off a series of clicks but one steady note that increased in pitch and intensity the nearer it was to the transmitter. It also gave a visual reading on a scale calibrated in hundreds of yards. I rented a pair of walkie-talkies, too, just in case. Phil threw in for nothing a second large receiving set that he had stripped of its innards so only the black outer box remained, complete with leather carrying strap. Money changed hands, from mine to his, then I picked up the freeway again and headed downtown to the new stone-clad edifice that housed the L A P D Central record department, amongst other things. Such as Tony, when he was working.

However I knew he was off that day as I knew where he was and it wasn't in downtown L A – he'd taken everyone up to Santa Barbara for the weekend to visit Mom's cousin Vi, which was why I'd taken Mom to Tony and Gaye on Friday instead of Sunday, our usual swapping-over time. Vi lived in a mobile home, and drank. There is not necessarily any connection.

In a clean, sweet-smelling, quiet room down in the first basement, the antithesis of what a room in a police station usually looks, smells and sounds like, I found Sid Myers, also known as Sneezy, a long-term friend and co-worker of Tony's and also a more than nodding acquaintance of mine. He was

a cantankerous, harassed little sod who had to work weekends and overtime as he had one of the most expensive hob-
bies known to man – marriage. No one minded his grumpy
nature however as he was a genius at his job.

Sid looked up from his console when I wandered in and
gave me his usual look of pain and high dudgeon, he reminded
me of that small redhead who was always in a frenzy of rage
against Bugs Bunny. And that small redhead reminded me of
that Scotsman who was always in a frenzy of rage against
Laurel and Hardy.

'Good afternoon, Sneezy,' I said brightly.

'It was,' he said, 'up to now. It was also a brilliant and
starry eve the night the *Titanic* sailed. What are you doing
here, anyway, you're not even supposed to be in here.'

'I need the help of the mighty LAPD record section,' I
said, 'in order to combat crime and evil-doing.'

'Save it,' he said. 'I've heard it all before.'

'Maybe not this one,' I said. I told him briefly about Mr
Lubinski's unusual problems.

'So what's it got to do with me?' he said. 'And what'cha
got in there, a contribution to my next alimony payment?' He
was referring to the envelope I was holding containing the
jewelry box.

'Italian fingerprints, I hope,' I said. 'Any chance you can
run it through the machine for me?'

Sid hemmed and hawed, as was to be expected, but he
finally took me next door where a pretty lady technician he
didn't bother to introduce me to dusted the box, lifted a set
of prints, photographically transferred them to a sensitized
sheet of pink paper about eight inches by ten, put them
through a kind of toaster, then handed the result back to
Sneezy, all of which took her some five minutes.

'Step one,' Sid said.

I followed him back to his desk. He slipped the sheet into a
slit in a shoe-box size piece of hardware, typed busily on his

console, then a perfect image of the prints came up in green on the screen.

'Step two,' he said. He went over to a file cabinet, unlocked it, and brought back a handful of floppy disks, one of which he fed into his computer. He did some more tapping to enter the prints into the memory system, and asked for a run. He got a match on the second run, then switched on the printer, which as you all probably know by now operates sort of like a teletype, but faster. It hammered away for some twenty seconds, then stopped. Sid tore off the printed sheet and handed it to me:

Luigi (Louis) Bellini.

AKA Little Lou. B. 4 July 1960 Orange NJ. M. Marion M. (d). F. Luigi G. (d). PA 4453 B St Orange NJ. LKA Apt 42 Quincey Arms Bourne BLVD Inglewood CA . . .

1974–76 Adams Juv. Home, Jersey City. 1977 – con. AR, 14 mos of 2 yrs served Dannamorra, NY. 1981 – AR EM – PB – Prob. 1981 – AR, EM, dis. 1983 – AR GBH, cd. KA: Maureen Larosa, aka Red, ad. sm. Antonio Gardino, aka Tony Garden. MORE FBI/22B/43/C. CLOSE.

Which, roughly translated, meant that Little Lou had been a bad boy, had done time twice, once in a juvenile home, had plea bargained once and walked, was up for extorting with menaces and got off, was up for grievous bodily harm and had the case dismissed, more than likely the victim declining to testify as he preferred grievously hurt to grievously dead.

Sid, who didn't miss much, said, 'Tony Garden.'

I said, 'You're telling me, Sneezy,' thanked him effusively and got out of there. See why I love computers? In the old days it would have taken weeks to check one odd set of prints for enough points of similarity against, say, a quarter of a million other sets, to say nothing of having to wire them to all the other police forces and federal agencies in the country and wait to see what they could come up with. Had it been the old days, I would have stealthily found out Lou's name to start with, which would have made it easier, but today, hell, you only need half a thumbprint and a computer terminal. Tony told me they can pretty much do the same thing with a photo now, especially if it's sharp and shows at least one ear, but that wasn't the main reason I'd brought Scoop Sara the kid reporter and her trick camera into it.

If Little Lou was a bad boy I don't know what you'd call Tony Garden, whom the print-out had simply listed as one of Lou's KAs, or known accomplices, but who was certainly Lou's employer-capo. A very bad boy, or a very naughty boy indeed, doesn't seem quite strong enough. Serious trouble is more like it, from what I heard. One of the two big drug chains was his, and I don't mean Rexall, most of the white hotel hooker action was his, Star Cars Taxis was his, a dozen escort services were his, half of the numbers action in most white areas of LA was his, Acme Construction, which laid more roads in California than any other two companies, was his, and God knows how much real estate, how many bookies, how many linen services, how many cops and how many robbers. To sum it up, Mr Garden was to be dealt with extremely carefully, if at all, and preferably at a considerable distance.

However who am I but an extremely careful fellow; I not only let Boy Scouts help me across busy thoroughfares but never never go out in the rainy season without a hanky and rubbers. And I did have a plan, or most of one.

On the way back uptown I stopped at Moe's for a couple of franks, mustard and relish only, and a root beer, and sweet-talked Son of Moe, who was sucking sugar, as usual, into letting me use his phone which wasn't supposed to be used by customers. The first call I made was to Mr Lubinski. He must have been lurking near his phone because he answered it almost before it rang.

'Lubinski, Lubinski and Levi,' he said. 'Good afternoon.'

'Good afternoon,' I said. 'This is your friendly travel agent calling. Time to lock up your valuables and pack your bags, Mr Lubinski, Philadelphia awaits.'

'Not only am I already packed,' he said, 'I've already left. Goodbye.'

'Got a number where you're going?' I said. 'I'll call you in a week or so, with any luck it'll be all over by then.'

'And without luck?' he said. 'I don't got a number but I've got a name.' He gave me his brother's name and address in South Philly, which I wrote down on a slightly used paper napkin. 'Luck,' he said bitterly. 'If I had any luck, would I be going to Philadelphia in winter? To my brother Mort's?'

I laughed and hung up. Then, as it was coming up to two o'clock and there was an outside chance my pal Benny might be awake, I gave him a ring.

He was up and delighted to hear from me, or so he said.

I asked him if he wanted to buy some gold.

He said, no, but he knew somebody who might want to buy some, how much did I have?

I told him. The amount didn't faze him for a moment.

How much was I asking?

'Two hundred and seventy-five dollars an ounce,' I said, adding, for purposes that will be revealed later, twenty-five dollars per ounce on top of the Italian's asking price.

'Seems very reasonable,' he said. 'Are you sure you've got your figures right?'

'Yes,' I said. 'I am sure. Benny, just out of curiosity, who would your potential customer be?'

He told me; I recognized the name, it was one of the names of a Chinese gentleman who had roughly the same status among LA's Orientals as Tony Garden did among the whites and for roughly the same reasons.

'What would he want it for?'

'Teeth,' said Benny. 'Do you know how many gold teeth there are walking around Chinatown and Little Korea and Little Vietnam?'

'No,' I said, 'of course I don't. How would I know? Benny, why wouldn't my guy sell direct to your guy?'

Benny thought for a moment. 'Is your guy perhaps of Italian hue?'

'Perhaps,' I said, 'if "hue's" the right word.'

'That's why,' he said. 'They don't mix. They hate each other. It's worse than Romeo and Juliet or the Hatfields and the McCoys or Jews and Arabs, you name it. I mean they do not get on. Their idea of friendly relations is total war.'

'Ah,' I said. 'Benny, you know any of the names your guy trades under, more or less legally?'

'Sure,' he said, and he rattled off a half a dozen, including the Far East Trading Company. 'It'll take a while to set it up at this end, my friend, even if my guy is interested, because you better believe I'll go through at least two cut-outs, there's no way I'm talkin' to those guys direct about that much gold.'

'I hear you,' I said. 'It'll take me a few days too, for slightly different reasons. So I'll get back to you when I can.'

Fine by him, he said. He gave me a post office box number where any communications of a sensitive nature could be safely addressed. He wanted to know if I had any spare time during the weekend as I was well overdue for a humiliation at the chess board; at one time he'd thrashed me regularly a couple of times a week but due to this and that, mostly that, I hadn't been by his nondescript Hollywood apartment for a while. I told him that quite frankly I had a lot more important things to do right then than play some childish game but I'd let him know. Before I hung up I asked him if he had a lot on next week. He said, no, not a lot, odds and ends, bits and pieces, you know me.

I did indeed. Benny's odds and ends might include anything from some slick new variation on pyramid selling to peddling space in trade directories of which there was only one copy, one he'd printed himself. Once he sold the same house three times although to be fair it was his house to begin with. He told me once he started as a mere youth selling color portraits of US presidents, by mail, for a buck. His customers got a one-cent stamp. Then he sold again by mail and again for a buck, a guaranteed system of making money. The system you got was to put a small-ad in a paper or comic that said, send me a buck and I'll send you a system guaranteed to make you money. Kid stuff, really, but you still see them today. He told me he'd once lived for a year selling tickets to bus tours, only he didn't have a bus or a tour, all he had was a cap, a badge and some tickets. He told me he used to make the odd fiver selling copies of special keys that open up those automatic machines on street corners that vend newspapers. He told me a lot of things, but that's enough for now.

Onwards. Onwards to Mrs Martel's stationery store next to the post office, where I nipped in first to look up the address of the Far East Trading Company. I told Mrs Martel, a short, arch woman wearing sequined glasses held on by a flashy gold chain, that business was so good I had to start another company. Two, in fact.

She nodded knowingly.

'And what are we to call our companies this time, Mr Daniel? The FBI? The California Committee for Unwed Mothers? The US Immigration Service? The California State Tax Department, Carmel Branch?' How she remembered these examples from my checkered past I'll never know.

I looked shocked. 'We are simply going to call them the Near East Trading Company and the Far East Trading Company,' I said.

'And I suppose we'll need both headed paper and matching headed envelopes again, medium bond?'

'You read my mind, darling,' I said.

'Lino or offset?' she said.

'Offset,' I said. 'And by the way, all this is in aid of, or at least I hope it will aid, a certain amazing gent called Mr

Lubinski, sometimes known as Solly, who is right now, I believe, on his way to visit relatives back East.'

'I know,' she said, reddening slightly. 'He dropped in to say goodbye.'

'Well!' I said. She dealt with a customer while I looked over her selection of maps, then she took me out back where her chinless son Geoffry held sway. I don't know if you care, but offset was the greatest invention in printing circles since Herr Gutenberg's original system of individual letters clamped together in rows, which you then inked and then pressed on a sheet of paper. With offset, you don't need thousands of individual letters in all the different typefaces. All you do is run your typed material through a machine that is basically a copier and it produces, given another easy step or two, the plate you ink up and print from. Suffice it to say that twenty minutes later I was out on the street again with two sets of twenty-four copies each of professionally printed, headed notepaper and matching envelopes. (I always had a few extras made up, it cost but pennies and one never knew.) I also had a map of South-Central California so I could track down Carmen Springs, where something called Tim's Tavern could be found.

And, I devoutly hoped, two of their regular customers, Dell and his brother, whoever he was. 'Asshole,' Tommy had called him: not a bad name for the kid.

CHAPTER FOURTEEN

Back at the office, I scribbled some rough notes, got the electric typewriter from the safe and was looking up the address of the head office of Acme Construction (CAL) Ltd when Sara came in and tossed her latest work of art on my desk.

'Here. You said you needed it right away.'

'Did I? Oh, yeah. Nice coat.' I gave an admiring whistle. She was wearing something that trailed on the floor and looked like it was left over from the Zulu Wars.

'Well? Aren't'cha gonna read it? Oh. I brung ya something else, as you're my favorite creep.' She dug in one pocket and produced a couple of crumpled oatmeal cookies wrapped in a Kleenex. 'Made by me,' she said proudly, as if oatmeal cookies were hard to make and anyway they were the bumpy normal kind, not the flat, brittle, golden-brown ones I really liked. I nibbled on one of the things to give her pleasure and skimmed through her 'report' while she puffed at one of those long women's cigarettes that look like cigars to try and calm her nerves. If there's anything I hate it's reading something of a so-called artistic nature in front of the person who wrote it. You'd think she was exposing her poor fragile soul in every badly typed line:

CONFIDENTIAL

17 Jan.
Report
From: Agent S.S.
To: V.D. (Ha ha)
(From notes taken in field)

8.45 a.m.

Left office of V.D. after briefing and instruction in use of
Spy camera. Nifty gadget, height (or depth?) of sneakiness,
Le voyeur's special.

8.50 a.m.

Purchased spiral notebook and Rapidwriter pen

Expenses $2.51.

From lippy lady in paper store across from L.L. & L.

A gift, are they? she says, implying, I suppose, that I was
Completely illiterate. If she only knew.

8.55 a.m.

Arrived at L.L. & L. (Address on request.)

L., mucho nervioso, let me in. Dropped small box he was
polishing twice.

I says, calm down, sir, the coward tastes of death a thousand
times,

The valiant never tastes of death but once. A poetic quote.

If I dealt in candles, the sun would never set, he says. A
Yiddish quote.

Snapped a few snaps. Jotted a few jots.

Asked him why he was polishing already polished box.

He told me.

Began to interview him properly to sink into my role,

Also to take his mind off things.

Did you know he was born in Estonia?

Did you know he had an operation on his prostate two years
ago?

Did you know girls don't have prostates?

Do you know he speaks a bissel Yiddish, whatever that
means?

9.40 a.m. (about)

Think I spot large, furtive private eye sneaking into health-
food bar

Across the street. Can't be right, from the look of him he's
never been

Near one of those places in his life.

9.55 a.m. (about)

Enter Greaseball. Yecch. Fake tan, shirt open to his curlies, gold

Medallion the size of a hubcap, basketweave shoes.

Almost made me prefer the Hawaiian look.

Musclebound, oozing oil and slippery yeech.

Sees me ever so vivacious, ever so questioning, and pretends interest

In a display of cufflinks.

L. hangin' in there. Be right with you, sir,

He says, this young lady (!)'s just finishing up her interview with me

For her school paper.

Then I snap off a few last shots, including I'm positive some beauties of Il Greaseballo.

You tell your teacher Lubinski is always glad to help, L. says.

Greaseball drifts to back of store as

I drift to front with L. Using L. as blocker, I neatly pocket

Cufflink box Greaseball has handled, taking L. off the hook.

Pose L. for final shot in front of his store.

See in reflection huge furtive private eye sneaking hurriedly off

Down the street,

Inconspicuous as dog doo on a white carpet.

10.05 a.m.

Report back to office of V.D.

Take that,

Sez Sara S.   Total Expenses $2.51

'Terrific,' I said when I'd finished. 'Most amusing. I think I have a right to go into that health-food bar if I want to, they happen to have excellent fresh orange juice there, I'm almost a regular.'

　　'Did I get him?' she asked. 'I thought I nailed the sucker.'

She tapped her ash in the wastepaper basket.

'Use the ashtray,' I said. 'Yeah, you got him, and we got a make on his prints, too.'

'Who is he? Show me the pictures.'

I showed them to her. 'He's a hood called Little Lou who's been arrested even more times than you've had weird hair-cuts,' I said.

'So what was he doing to Mr Lubinski, who was terrific, you were right.'

What the hell, it couldn't hurt, so I told her about it. Her drawn-on eyebrows went way up.

'What are you going to do to the big shit?'

'I can't do much to the big shit,' I said, 'but I'm hoping to persuade his boss, who makes the big shit look like Joan of Arc, to take his business somewhere else.'

'How?' She came around to my side of the desk and looked at my scribbled notes. I didn't dissuade her as I hoped she might for once forget the measly expense money I owed her if I kept her preoccupied.

'There are two things I want,' I told her. 'Mr Lubinski out of it and no one mad at either him or me. There are three things the big shit's boss wants, because I know the type, to make money, to get respect and to get his own way. So, I am going to write him a very polite, respectful letter suggesting a way that he can make more money by not using Mr Lubin-ski.'

'I'll help,' she said eagerly. 'I'm a writer, a lot better writer than you are, you've probably never written a poem in your life.'

'I have too,' I said. 'I wrote one on a valentine card once, I remember it to this day. "Roses are red, they have a nice smell. I wish I could say, your feet do as well." Anyway, you've probably never written a letter to a Mafia capo in your life. But, O K, scoot your chair over here but don't bug me.'

130

She dragged her chair around to my side and then for some reason hit me on the arm a couple of times.

'Grow up, will you,' I said.

'Look who's talking,' she said.

First, I addressed the envelope to Mr Garden.

'How'd you get his address?' she asked.

'Phone book.'

'How do you know he'll be there?'

'He owns the company,' I said. 'So I figure he drops in from time to time to count the petty cash.'

'Who's the Near East Trading Company?'

'It doesn't exist,' I said, rolling a sheet of paper into the machine.

'Why?'

'Use your head,' I said, 'for something else than growing cooties. The last thing I want is for those madmen to know I'm involved. But it should look and sound like it's coming from a legitimate company.'

'Why that name?'

'Sort of a joke,' I said. 'Sort of an attention-grabber.'

'Why P O Box 44767, Fresno, C A?' she then asked. It was of course the address Benny had given me.

'It's a cut-out,' I said.

'What's a cut-out?'

'Like a dead end. It was set up by a friend of mine. A letter goes there, it goes inside another envelope, then it goes somewhere else. Can I get on with it?'

'Be my guest,' she said. 'Mean typewriter you got there.'

Dear Mr Garden (we, but mostly me, wrote):
Do you sincerely want to be richer?

I represent a syndicate that has recently become aware of your interest in the prevailing price of gold. May I say at this time that our organization, the Near East Trading Company, has no connection with anyone who might be operating under a similar name, such as the Far East Trading Company.

May I respectfully draw your attention to the following:

(a) Mr Lubinski, of Lubinski, Lubinski and Levi, Family Jewelers for over Twenty Years, being unable to withstand recent business pressures, has decided to sell out and, with his charming wife, fulfill a long-standing dream by emigrating to Israel. They are actually on the first leg of their trip as I write this; their (well-insured) premises vacated, their valuable stock removed for safekeeping to a bank.

(b) These business pressures referred to were of course applied by one of your employees, Mr Luigi Bellini, aka Little Lou, who has had a good deal of previous experience in this line. (Details on request, courtesy LAPD Record Department and the FBI.)

(c) We have in our possession both the testimony of two independent witnesses plus a written deposition from Mr Lubinski placing Mr Bellini in the store, as well as several candid snaps of him conversing with Mr Lubinski, one of which I am pleased to enclose.

(d) We have a recording of the entire conversation between Mr Lubinski and Mr Bellini made during Mr Bellini's second visit to the store, the highly illicit nature of which you can well imagine. (Copy on request.)

Here Sara interrupted me by saying, 'I didn't know you were bugging him too.'

'I wasn't,' I said, 'but if we got his prints and his picture we obviously could have. Onwards.'

(e) Both of us would, I am sure, prefer not to involve Mr Bellini and, by implication, yourself, in any way, with the law.

(f) We have an alternative buyer for your merchandise, Mr Lubinski now being unavailable.

(g) This buyer will pay $25 an ounce *more* than the price agreed on by Mr Lubinski and will take unlimited quantities.

(h) I suggest, therefore, with respect, it would be to both our advantages if you dealt directly with us in this matter. With our joint experience I have no doubt we could come up with a delivery and payment system that would protect and satisfy us both.

Yours sincerely,

Arthur M. Schindler (Pres)

Then I borrowed Sara's new pen and signed it with a flourish.

'What was all that about well-insured premises and the bank?' she asked me.

'Obvious, chérie,' I said. 'You're dealing with people who not only don't mind violence, but adore it. I'm just trying my humble best to prevent them chucking bombs around or driving cement trucks through the Lubinski front window.'

'So what'll happen when he comes back in a couple of weeks and opens up again?'

'So his wife couldn't stand Israel,' I said patiently. 'Who could plan on that?'

'Me,' she said.

I tucked the letter and one of the prints in the envelope and rummaged around for a stamp.

'Know something?' she said, wandering over to look at my meager collection of reading material.

'Yeah,' I said. 'You got a hole in your stocking.'

'They're tights,' she said, 'and it's on purpose, where've you been? I was gonna say, it might work.'

'Like me,' I said. 'I might work if you got out of here and let me. Where did I put those Goddamned stamps? I just bought them.'

'You need a secretary,' she said.

'Oh no I don't,' I said.

'They're probably right under your nose,' she said, wandering back my way. 'Men are so helpless sometimes.' I didn't even bother to answer that old slander. 'And what is this for?' She snatched up an envelope from the desk where I'd been piling up the contents of my stationery drawer because I knew I had some stamps in there somewhere.

'The Far East Trading Company,' she read. 'Is that you too?'

'No, my dear,' I said, snatching the envelope back, 'that is mayhap for some rainy day when I want to start a small war.'

'Between who and who?'

'Try Italy and China,' I said. 'Now beat it. On second thought, don't beat it. You don't have a pal who's got a camper, do you?' I finally found the stamps in my shirt pocket and stuck one on.

She thought for a minute, then said no.

'Goin' somewhere?' She found a small stack of business cards and was riffling through them. 'Verrrrry interesting!' she exclaimed, holding up one. 'V. Daniel, Inspector Building Codes and Violations, Venice, California. You do get around.'

'Mind your own business,' I said. 'Give me those.' I swept everything off the desk and back into the drawer, which I locked. 'Yes, I am going somewhere. I am going north. Want to come?'

'How far north, Iceland?'

'Not quite that far, little one.'

'For how long?'

'A couple of days.'

'Just us?' She had the nerve to leer at me.

'No way,' I said. 'With a Nicaraguan guy I know. And maybe Benny.'

She took out some purple lipstick and began smearing it in the general area of her mouth.

'Do I get paid?' she asked.

'Sure.'

'Danger money?'

'Where do you get all that rubbish?' I said. 'There is no such thing as danger money.'

'God you're cheap,' she said. 'You never even paid me for my last job, let alone the expenses I forked out. That's two fifty-one, buster, and I could have got killed, you told me so yourself, even you were worried otherwise what were you doing lurking around?'

'Having an important business appointment in the neighborhood can hardly be called lurking around,' I said huffily. 'Anyway, it's your choice. You can get paid by the hour or by the job like the illiterate menial a complete stranger took you for not so long ago, or you can get paid by the month like real professionals and executives and leaders of industry.'

'Give,' she said, holding out the ungloved of her two hands, a grubby affair that had five rings on one finger and none on any of the others. I dug, I gave, willingly, is not the laborer worthy of her hire, even this laborer?

'OK,' she said, 'now we can start talkin' about next week.' She examined with squinted eyes the perfectly good five-dollar bill I'd just given her, among others. 'I bet it's got something to do with that guy whose phone we bugged, am I right? Can we talk?'

I admitted she was, for once, not wrong.

'You better ask my mom though. I dunno if she'd let me go otherwise. She should be at home unless she's gone shopping.'

So I called Mrs Silvetti, Sara's (adoptive) Mom. We'd talked on the phone a few times before and I'd met her once when Sara brought her by the office to show her I was real. It seemed that her parents had trouble believing that anyone remotely sane would pay their daughter real money to work for him. Of course neither Sara nor I bothered to tell Mom the precise nature of the occasional tasks she performed for me.

I told Mrs Silvetti I wanted to borrow her daughter for a few days as I had a rather boring but complicated insurance claim to look into and as it involved a teenage girl who'd been hurt in an automobile accident I thought having a young girl of my own along might help. It sounded weak even to me but Mrs Silvetti said it was fine with her if it was all right with her husband and it would be all right with her husband as they both thought I was a good influence on their girl. Little did they know.

Then I put things away, locked up, dropped the letter in the corner box, waved to Mrs Morales, then we drove out Victory past the film studios to a used-car lot I dealt with as it had everything from the latest models to panel trucks to old clunkers to classics to dump trucks, you name it. They had a row of campers out back; the guy in the office said they were all open, have a look, and if I wanted to try any of them, come back for the keys.

'Know anything about campers?' I asked Sara, who had stopped to sneer at a gorgeous old Plymouth, a 48, in light and dark brown, original chrome, it made your mouth water to just look at it.

'No,' she said. 'Jesus, they sure made piles of shit in those days. You know anything about them?'

'Enough,' I said. 'Pop used to have one but I can only remember us ever taking one trip in it, then the shocks or something went and he sold it.'

There was one camper in the line I thought might do. It was a Volks conversion but with an extra bit built over the driver's seat where kids could sleep, leaving their folks the two bunks at the back.

'Where's the john?' she wanted to know.

'Already?' I said. 'There.' I pointed through the sliding door to the great outdoors.

'Gross,' she said.

I showed her where the gas ring had been cunningly hidden, likewise the small sink, and how the table folded up, then looked in the cupboards in case some fool had left some staples behind or at least the odd pot and pan. They hadn't. Then I showed her how the cute gingham curtains slid back and forth.

'Sick-making,' she said. 'Is this trip really necessary?'

I borrowed the keys from the front office, started it up and took it for a spin around the yard; the valves didn't sound quite right but otherwise it seemed OK. I told the guy who was minding the store I'd take it for a few days starting Monday, gave him a deposit, took one last yearning glance at the Plymouth, then drove Sara back to her place.

'See ya,' she said, scrambling out. 'Don't think it hasn't been, cause it hasn't.'

'Sure hasn't,' I agreed. 'Oh. One more thing, I almost forgot, on the trip, guess what. You get to call me Daddy.'

I drove sedately off, as befitting a new father.

CHAPTER FIFTEEN

It was late Sunday morning. I had things to do – lists to make, people to call, plans to lay, stuff to buy – so I made the calls, to Mom, Sara, Ricky, Benny and Evonne, then let my wayward darling talk me into letting her take me to the beach. There was a boat broker I vaguely wanted to talk to who usually hung around the pier at Manhattan Beach, but he wasn't there so we did what there is to do in January at the beach – not much.

We strolled out to the end of the pier and watched people not catching fish. We strolled along the boardwalk, although in Manhattan Beach it is a cement walk, eating rubbish and talking same, at least from my end. Held hands. I bought her a copper bent-wire brooch that said 'Evonne' that we watched being bent before our very eyes. She bought me a T-shirt that said 'Italians Do It Better'. Saw a bartender I used to know, Morrie, from the Coach and Horses, years ago, who had since gone straight, if you call selling to tourists over-priced shell ashtrays with little plastic palm trees glued on them, going straight. Evonne stopped to pop her eyeballs at some bodybuilders who were working out in a fenced playpen near the tennis courts.

'Wow!' she said.

I, for once, wisely said nothing.

And so the day passed, and the evening, which we spent together, and the night, which we also spent together. When I left her place in the morning, Monday morning, I was wearing my new T-shirt but it didn't do a lot for me except tell it like it was.

Back home, I made myself a mug of coffee, wrote up some

detailed notes for Benny, then began rounding up the equipment, provisions and clothes I thought I might need during the next few days, starting with the most important things first: 1 hand gun, Police Positive, .38 cal., taped grip; 1 box cartridges for same; 2 pairs of cheap handcuffs, with keys; 1 pacifier/cosh/blunt instrument (roughly, a tube of soft leather sewed up at both ends and filled with ball bearings); 1 sheath knife; 1 Swiss Army knife; 2 flares; camera and flash; 5-battery flashlight; 1 mustache; 1 pair shades. Then came things like boots and rainwear, sleeping bags, binoculars, an old army poncho. Then came the apparatus from Phil at J & M's Home Security, then some assorted kitchenware. Then I popped out to Ralph's for bottled gas for the camper stove, some food and some 80-proof snakebite remedy, brandy-flavored, not forgetting a couple of six-packs of beer. I got back just in time to let in the troops, who arrived right on noon, as we'd arranged Sunday by phone. First came Benny, in his Dodge Colt, then Ricky in the Wagoneer right behind him. Sara we'd pick up on the way.

My pal Benny looked inoffensive, as usual, with his baby face and blue eyes. He'd dressed for the part he was to play in tan chinos, matching jacket, L A Dodgers baseball cap and a pair of square, steel-rimmed glasses. He was toting a Y M C A holdall containing his extra clothes. Ricky was wearing his official working uniform.

'Any trouble this morning?' I asked him as soon as we all got upstairs.

'Nada,' he said. 'I had this friend of ours, Mrs Gonzales, drive me out to work cause I'd left the car out there and as soon as Tommy took off so did I and here I am. By the way, I'm Ricky,' he said to Benny.

'Benny,' said Benny. They shook hands. I gave Benny the notes I'd written up for him and he looked through them while Ricky ran down for me the equipment he'd brought along – 1 Colt Cobra with holster, ammo, flash, plus the survival belt he always wore in the woods. Then he handed me a check for a sizable amount of money. I didn't want to take it but he said I'd better, it came from Ellena's emergency fund and she wouldn't take no for an answer, you know her. I said I did and I would keep it in case we couldn't finance the operation some other way.

Then we had a general discussion of tactics, then some more coffee, then I herded them out, all of us well laden, locked up, then we went down and loaded up the Jeep. I went back in for a moment to have a quick word with Feeb, my landlady downstairs. I told her if anyone asked, I'd be away for a couple of days fishing with some friends.

'You and whose army?' she said. 'According to your mother, all you know about fish is you don't like them unless they're pickled in sour cream.'

I gave her a friendly pat on the top of her blue rinse, then we took off. At the used-car lot we transferred all my gear to the camper, I settled up with the man in the front office, then I led the parade to Sara's. She was ready, which was a mild surprise, in fact she was sitting outside her apartment building on the steps, a bulging, bright orange knapsack beside her. I do not know what she was dressed for, a costume party perhaps at Alice Cooper's, but she certainly wasn't wearing what a normal girl would put on for a few days' camping holiday with her father, even a temporary father. Red gauchos, what looked like argyle golf socks, high-heeled half boots with pointed toes, the kind I believe the Limeys call winklepickers, lime-green turtleneck ten sizes too large and a man's tweed vest. Blue sunglasses with only one lens left. Red sun visor. Black lipstick. White gloves with all the fingers cut off. A veritable cover girl for the *Saturday Evening Punk*.

Benny got out of the camper to open the sliding door for her, a gesture of politeness I admit didn't occur to me.

I said, 'Benny, Sara.'

He said, 'Charmed.'

She said, 'Likewise, I'm sure.'

They both climbed in, Benny beside me and what's-her-name in the back, then I signalled Ricky, who was parked right in front of us, with a toot on the horn, and off we went with Ricky in the lead as he knew the way, he'd actually been to Carmen Springs once, or close enough, anyway, he'd told me.

We filled up with gas before hitting the freeway, then headed north up the San Fernando Valley, the old familiar route that led to Wonderland Park, Parson's Crossing, and, more or less, Mohave, Modesto and ultimately, if you went far enough, Sacramento.

As soon as Sara was settle she rapped me on one shoulder, the one that was still sore thanks to Lefty Donovan, and said, 'OK, Grumps, what's goin' on?'

'Yes, Uncle,' Benny chimed in. 'Tell all.' Benny, of course, thought it was amusing to call me Uncle because I'd almost married his Aunt Jessica that time. I didn't think it was amusing, and had told him so a million times at least.

'Don't call me Uncle,' I said wearily one more time. 'And you, Burrhead, to you I'm Daddy, if you don't mind.'

'Yeccch,' she said.

'I'll be happy to tell you all when we've got Ricky with us,' I said, 'then I won't have to go over it twice.'

'Who's Ricky?' Sara wanted to know.

'Ahead of us, in that station wagon thing,' Benny said, pointing.

'Oh,' she said. 'That's Ricky.' A minute later she said, 'Anyone want a joint?'

'Don't mind,' said Benny. So my brave troops got smashed and discussed weighty matters like crunchy vs. smooth peanut butter and Rocky Road vs. butterscotch-swirl ice cream, leaving me with naught to do but drive and muse and occasionally ponder about truly important matters like copper wire, needle-nose pliers, brooches that said 'Evonne' and girls, or at least one girl, who, when she got up to get a drink of water in the night, not only brought you one as well but fed it to you like you were a baby.

We stayed on the freeway tootling along in the slow lane some sixty miles before turning off to pick up an eastbound secondary road which took us through such well-known towns as Opeka, Boliches and Sand Hill. When, according to a road sign, we were eleven miles out of Carmen Springs, I tooted to get Ricky's attention and hand signaled him to pull over. He found a lane a few hundred yards further on and turned into it and stayed on it until it took a twist and we couldn't be seen from the main road anymore. Then we all piled out and took a few breaths of mild, sweet, country air.

Actually, it was damp country air and it wasn't that sweet because somewhere lurking invisibly in the neighborhood was either a tannery or a sugar-beet refinery or maybe it was a pulp mill. Anyway, we took a few breaths of it, I introduced Sara to Ricky, cracked open a six-pack from the cooler, we arranged ourselves more or less comfortably on the grass verge, then I looked sternly at my troops and declared the council of war open.

As Sara and Benny had little idea of what had gone on already, and as all three of them had little idea of what was ahead of us, I took it from the top, as the hipsters say, only omitting for sake of brevity some of the more boring details like the llama bite and being sick on the fire-tower ladder.

I told them about the missing merinos, or rather Suffolks, my clever deductions about a possible culprit, my meeting with Ricky and his amigo Tommy DeMarco, the visit to Chico's, and so on. I briefly sketched in the reasoning that led me to suspect Tommy, told them about the call to Sheriff Gutes, and how Sara and a willing boy had bugged Tommy's phone.

The troops listened with gratifying attention.

'So what we are up against is, at least, a man called Dell

and his no-name brother who frequent Tim's Tavern, in Carmen Springs just up the road there. The brother has killed at least one man we know about, pobre Chico. We suspect the two of them grow and deal an awful lot of good weed, meaning big money. Which means they and God knows how many others they're mixed up with, outside of Tommy, are highly dangerous. Which means we are not on a picnic, men. And woman. Which is why we've stopped here, well out of town. We don't know where Dell and his brother live. They could be driving past us on that main road right now and I don't want them to see us together yet. I want to keep Ricky and you, Benny my boy, out of it until I need you. Sara and me, we go into town together. We park at Tim's Tavern. We go in. We're looking for a spot to put the camper for a few days, square old Dad, who they will soon find out is a private investigator, and his real juvenile delinquent daughter who he has removed from the den of sin called Los Angeles to try and straighten her out by showing her the beauties of nature and life in the raw and who is consequently greatly pissed off at him.'

'That won't be hard, Pop,' said Sara, looking around her with distaste.

'Right on,' I said. 'That's it, that's your attitude throughout.'

'And who's he?' Sara asked, throwing a clod of earth in Benny's lap.

'He's an electronics expert from the Sheriff's Department who comes in later,' I said. Benny smiled and made a small bow.

'And what am I doing during all this?' Ricky asked, taking another beer.

'You are being invisible, like Benny,' I said. 'Find a place to stay for a night or so somewhere close but not too close. You have the number of Tim's Tavern because I included it in Benny's notes. The first thing Sara does when we get to Tim's is to make a scene with me, then she makes a fake call to her doper boyfriend to whom she loudly gives the phone number of Tim's so he can call her back when he wants to. At six tonight she gets a call all right but it's you, Ricky. You give her the phone number where you are staying so we can get a hold of you when we want you. This is called establishing our lines of communication without arousing suspicion. O K so far, troops'

My troops nodded.

'Almost makes sense,' Sara admitted. She took out one of her Virginia Slims or whatever triumph of advertising they were. Ricky lit it for her, putting the spent match back in the box as he always did. Two crows flew overhead, took one look at us and continued on their way.

'But what is all this in aid of?' Benny asked. 'I mean, what is all this for?'

'I'll tell you what it's all for, Benny,' I said. I was uncomfortable on the ground, as I usually was, even without one stiff leg (bring up the violins here) so I got up and walked around a bit. 'We got a problem. We got one dead boy who could be buried anywhere in a million miles of jungle. How do we find him? That is our problem. Any ideas, anyone?'

Benny raised his hand as if he was in school.

'Yes, Benny.'

'What about a helicopter over-flight. If we went low enough, that plantation would stand out like a sore thumb.'

'It's expensive, if we rent our own helicopter and pilot,' I said. 'If it's one from the Sheriff's Department, then it's all out of our hands, and Ricky and I have a personal interest in those two. Also, that only gets us the pot plantation, how do we find Chico?'

'Also you're too chicken to fly in one of those things,' Sara put in unnecessarily. I didn't even bother to answer her.

'I tell you how we find Chico, man,' said Ricky grimly. 'I got an idea. We grab Dell or his brother or both and squeeze their balls off, perdóname, señorita, until they tell us.'

'Well, that's an idea all right,' I said. 'There are only several major faults in it. It might not work. These are tough dudes, they will resist, violently, being grabbed. They may even be tough enough to resist having their balls grabbed, perdóname, señorita.'

'Don't mind me,' said Sara. 'Just pretend I'm one of the boys like you usually do.' I gave her a falsely affectionate look.

'Also, Ricky, amigo,' I went on, 'are confessions obtained under duress legally valid? And can information received by torturing someone be used at all under our legal system? Remind me to send you a pamphlet on the subject sometime.'

'Who cares?' said Ricky, scowling.

'OK,' I said. 'So we kill them afterwards. You swore an oath, so did I, to get my license, we're not supposed to kill citizens unless under extreme conditions or self-defense.'

'Who cares?' Ricky repeated. 'I'll do it. It will be a pleasure.'

'No, it won't,' said Benny. 'Take my word on that.' I gave him a look of surprise; he seemed to be referring to some specific event he'd never mentioned to me.

'Listen,' I said. 'We're a highly noticeable group. Look at us. People will notice us. Tim of Tim's Tavern, if there is such a person, will notice us. His customers will notice us. And if you, Ricky, are around, they will notice you. If Dell and his brother suddenly disappear, someone's going to blow the whistle on us and then in comes the fuzz and out comes the whole story, or enough of it so that you, amigo, can say adios to the Forestry Department and probably adios to the US of A if enough of it comes out, like you harboring an illegal alien, let alone killing citizens. Am I getting through to you? Maybe you could kill the brother who killed Chico, but could you kill Dell if he had nothing to do with it, if he wasn't even there? You'd have to because he'd know all about you by then.'

'Talk about not being there,' said Sara, 'what if Dell and his brother are not here? I mean, here in Carmen Springs?'

'I'm not too worried about that,' I said. 'They'll be back sooner or later, when it's cool, and we could always find them from what we know now if we had to, it'll just be more convenient if they're still around now.'

'Well, let's hear your brilliant plan, then,' said Ricky, frowning and looking away.

'My plan is this,' I said. 'We let them lead us to Chico, then we grab them.'

'Why would they ever go near him again, for Christ's sake?' Ricky asked the air. 'He's six feet under covered with logs somewhere, why would they ever go near him again?'

'We give them a good reason,' I said.

'You do like to drag things out,' said Benny. 'What reason?' He was picking at his teeth with a blade of what my pop used to call timothy grass – and who knows, he could have been right; although he wasn't a great naturalist he could tell the difference between elderberry wine and Four Roses with his eyes closed.

'Best reason of all,' I said. 'Survival. Look. We show up at Tim's. So do they, sooner or later, we hope. Me in a mustache and shades. They know there's a huge, fat jerk, a nothing, unquote, looking into Chico's disappearance because Ricky told it to Tommy, and he told it to them on the phone.'

'A perfect description, if you ask me,' said Sara.

'Nobody did,' I said. 'How long do you think it'll take before Dell and his brother start wondering if there is any connection between that fat huge jerk and the new fat huge jerk who's suddenly on the scene supposedly camping out with his airhead daughter?'

'Not too long,' said Benny.

'Like the speed of light,' said Sara.

'And in the unlikely chance that they don't tumble,' I said, 'my loving daughter will soon accidentally on purpose spill the beans because she's mad at Daddy.'

'So?' said Ricky.

'So,' I said. 'They call up Tommy and describe me. "Well,

except for the stash and the glasses, that could be the mother," says Tommy. "You want to come up here and take a look?" they ask him. "You must be out of your mind," he says. "I'm not going near you guys." I'm paraphrasing, you understand. So what do they do? They try and find out if the big jerk is accidentally up there with his daughter or if he really knows something. So when I split the friendly scene at Tim's early one evening, Sara tells her new drinking buddies her daddy's meeting someone who is sort of fuzz but not quite. And Tommy and the boys will want to know who that is because if it is Ricky, they've got real problems because the two fat jerks are one and the same and he is closing in. If it is someone else Daddy is meeting, it could have nothing to do with them. And if Tommy phones up Ricky at his home to see if he's there or not, the easy way to check, what does he get?'

'He gets Mrs Gonzales,' said Ricky, 'who's staying with us for a few days and who is answering all the calls. And who says, because she don't speaka de English so well, oh, the señor and señora and la chiquita are maybe at la clinica and maybe not, she's nota sure.'

'Thank you,' I said. 'What we want, ideally, is for either Dell or his bro or both of them to sneak up on our innocent camper that evening, whatever evening it is, and it will be easy sneaking as I'll park it somewhere close to some trees that makes it easy, and inside they will see, as the curtains won't be drawn, and hear, as the windows will be open, not Ricky, but Benny the boy electronics wonder with his bags of tricks, and me, plotting.'

'Plotting what?' said Sara impatiently.

'Their downfall,' I said. 'Benny, learn those notes I gave you because it'll be mostly up to you.' I fished the straggly mustache out of my pocket; it was the self-adhesive kind so I just pressed it in place. Then I put my shades on.

'The worst,' said Sara.

'Really?' I said. 'Come on, daughter, on your feet. It's show time.'

CHAPTER SIXTEEN

Ricky remembered to hand over some surveyor's maps I'd asked for, then the boys went one way, west, in the Jeep, and Sara and I eastward toward Carmen Springs in the camper. We drove past some green fields, then some brown fields, then a bright yellow one, then some more green ones. A dog appeared from nowhere and chased us for a bit. Two horses, a large one and a small one, turned their heads to watch us drive past. A kid hanging on a fence gave us a wave. Sara waved back, languidly but haughtily, as if she were the Queen of England.

'I'd hate to be him,' she said, 'stuck out here in the boonies, what kind of life is that? No one to talk to but sunflowers.'

'His daddy probably makes five times as much a year as yours does from those sunflowers,' I said.

'Still,' she said. She dismissed the whole idea with one impolite gesture. A few minutes later she said, 'Oh, Daddy.'

'Now what?'

'I'm gettin' nervous,' she said. 'I think I'm gonna toss my cookies.' She made a revolting noise in her throat which pleased her so much she made another, longer one. I decided the best thing to do with her was to ignore her, so I did.

'Mighty Carmen Springs,' she said a minute later, 'comin' up fast dead ahead. Looks like a lively place, if you like ghost towns.'

'Atta girl,' I said. 'Right in character.'

It wasn't exactly a ghost town but it is true to say Carmen Springs wasn't precisely jumping that Monday afternoon in January. Like many a similar small town, its function was to serve the surrounding farm community, not to provide fun and excitement at four thirty on a weekday afternoon. 'Pop: 1786 and growing fast' said a sign on the way into town. There was a surprisingly large general store with a US flag out in front, so I deduced it was also the local post office. A Five & Dime across from it. Drugstore. Clothing store with two show windows, one for work clothes. A farm machinery agency. Gas station, repair shop and junkyard, with a couple of rundown motel units out back. All-purpose meeting hall, movie house, church hall and what have you. A bridge over a lively stream, no doubt Carmen Spring itself.

'I wonder who Carmen was?' I said, pulling up at the town's one stoplight, which was of course against us.

'Who cares?' Sara said. 'There.' She pointed right in front of my face. 'Tim's Tavern.'

'I see it.' When the light changed some five minutes later, we crossed the intersection and coasted into Tim's parking lot. There were a few vehicles there already, an old Ford, a beat-up Datsun, a couple of well-used pick-ups. I looked over at the twerp.

'OK?'

'Let's hit it, Pops,' she said.

'Remember, first thing you do is get some change and phone LA,' I told her.

'I remember,' she said, clambering out her side. 'Jesus wept.'

I climbed out too, locked up, then had a good stretch. Tim's Tavern, from the outside, looked like any small-town bar – low, rectangular, made of unpainted cinderblock, neon beer ads in the windows. A large, hand-painted sign on the door made the welcome announcement that happy hour was from 4.30 to 7.00.

We went in. I always like going into a new bar. I like going into old ones too, but with new ones you can't help feeling there is always the outside chance of something unexpected happening, call it adventure, call it romance, call it what you will. In a small way, it's like seeing a big city for the first time, at night, when all the kindly lights hide the scars and the dirt. It was highly unlikely, however, that I for one would find any romance in Tim's Tavern, not of course that I was in the market those days, but it was highly possible we would find adventure of one kind or another.

And Tim's Tavern, from the inside, as well, looked like any small-town bar, but who would want it to look different – long bar on the right, shuffleboard game on the left, a few small tables in between. Farther back was a pool table, two pinball machines and a jukebox. The usual signs were stuck up behind the bar – 'Free Drinks Tomorrow' 'I have an agreement with my bank manager – I don't lend money and he doesn't sell alcohol' 'Drinking is a slow death – so who's in a hurry?' 'Work – the curse of the drinking classes' 'Don't ask me, ask the boss – my wife'.

The man behind the bar was small, red-cheeked and chirpy. He had an IHC cap on, a plaid shirt, red bow tie and bright crimson suspenders. A couple of farmer types were at one of the tables putting away shorts with beer chasers. An old-timer held down the corner stool at the far end of the bar, an empty beer glass in front of him. All four of them took one look at me when we came in, a longer one at Sara, then they all looked away again politely. Unless of course they didn't believe their eyes.

'Howdy,' I said genially to the assembly. One of the farmers nodded my way. I took a seat at the bar. 'Fred. Fred Perkins. And I had a daughter when I came in.' I looked around to see where the dope was, she was mooning about near the door. 'You Tim?'

'All my life,' the shorty behind the bar said. 'Get you folks something?'

'I could drink a glass of beer,' I admitted. 'What about you, Sara?'

'Yeccch,' she said. 'My idea of a perfect holiday, watching you drink beer.'

I gave a 'what can you do with kids today' look at Tim, who was putting a draft in front of me on a beer coaster. I took a long sip, smacked my lips, then said, 'Join me in something?'

He made a production of thinking it over, checked his watch, then allowed he might force down a light Seagram's and Seven. When he had poured himself the drink, he asked me if we were just passing through. I said it sort of depended, it looked like a pleasant part of the world, we might stay a day or two if I could find a place to stick the darn camper.

'Stick her all the way out back if you want,' Tim said, 'in them trees just off the tarmac. Won't nobody bother you there 'cepting the timber wolves and you got water just down the hill and most important of all, a short walk home after closing time.'

I ignored the bit about the wolves, figuring it was rustic wit, and thanked the man. Then Sara, who had been lounging about looking scornfully at the wall decorations, such as they were, came over, took a swig of my beer, then asked Tim if he had a phone. He said he had one last time he looked, right back there. She took out a soiled dollar bill that was rolled up in one of her half-gloves, got some change from Tim and mooched off toward the rear of the building. The two farmers almost wricked their necks in their well-mannered efforts not to stare at her as she passed their table.

I went after her and said firmly, 'Now, Sara, you are not to phone that no-good motorcycle punk what's-his-name, you hear me?'

'You know perfectly well what his name is,' she said. 'It's Rocky. And I'll call him if I want to.'

I looked helplessly after her, then sighed and went back to the bar where Tim had busied himself diplomatically with some unnecessary chore. I had a couple more beers, then Sara came back, ordered herself a Coke, took one sip, and left. Then the farmers paid their tab and left too. Tim took a free beer down the length of the bar to the old-timer. When he came back I asked him if he did any food.

'Burgers, dogs and chili,' he said. 'Also chili dogs and chili burgers. My own chili. But the grill's off til I get around to turning it on. Won't be long.'

I thanked him again, paid up, left a useful tip, and took myself out of there. I couldn't see any sign of my loving daughter so I got back in the camper and gave the horn a couple of toots. After a few minutes she appeared and climbed in beside me.

'Where you been, seeing the sights?' I asked her.

'Yeah,' she muttered. 'And, you've seen one Five & Dime, you've see 'em all. How'd I do in there?'

'Terrific,' I said. 'Just like a real daughter.'

I started up the motor and we drove as instructed out back of Tim's some fifty yards to where the paved area stopped and the trees started. By following some tracks that were already there in the grass we found the right spot. It was almost completely encircled by trees and some kind soul had even built a barbecue out of old cinderblocks and a piece of grill and left it there.

So we puttered around for an hour unpacking, connecting up the stove and the lamp, and wandering down to the stream. Sara made us some coffee that we drank black because I'd forgotten the milk and we got the sleeping bags laid out and all in all acted like the innocent greenhorns we were supposed to be, which wasn't hard.

At a few minutes before six we were back in Tim's. I was to cover the front of the bar and Sara to try and hang out at the back, near the phone to take Ricky's call and also to see if anyone was making or getting long-distance calls. Tim had some after-work business by then, enough for him to need a girl to help out – roughly half the customers were the overall trade and the others town folk, clerks and store owners, plus a table of housewives.

Right on six the phone rang and a lanky beanpole with a Pacific Bell shirt on who had been playing pool answered it, then shouted out, 'Is there a Sara in the house?'

'You better believe it, Shorty,' she told him, and bustled off to answer it. When she came back she gave me a nod which I took to mean that we had successfully established communications with the rest of the troops. Then she went off to shoot a game with Shorty while I kept my ears open unsuccessfully for anyone called Dell who had a brother.

After an hour I tried some of Tim's chili – it was fair, if you like chili that's all beans. Then I tried two of his chili dogs, hold the chili. They were fair. Then I had two pickled eggs that were great. Sara, of course, in her role of total nuisance, wouldn't eat anything. When I decided to call it quits for the night, she promptly decided she wanted to stay for a while and maybe pop a few with her new admirer, who was already somehow deeply within her thrall. I'd been afraid Tim or the waitress Maureen might hit on her for some ID, but it hadn't happened. People intelligently seem to be looser about such things in the sticks where kids of twelve and thirteen can often be found driving tractors and other farm machinery they're not legally supposed to, but who cares. In some states it's not even illegal if they stay on farm property; I don't know how I know that, but I do. I suspect it was one of the very few things I picked up when I did my time on a juvenile correctional farm back East. Two of the other things I picked up I no longer have, the ability to second deal and head lice.

I was sound asleep in my bunk when Sara came in a while later. She was thoughtful enough to keep the noise level down so that she only woke me up twice. The third time I woke up that night was when it started to rain and as I'd left the top vent up, water was splashing in on the floor between us. Guess who mopped it up?

*

Tuesday morning dawned clear but a mite breezy. After a quick cold-water wash-up, I locked the camper carefully and we took a stroll down the main street, which was called Main Street, where we had an indifferent breakfast at the Rosewood Grill. Then we looked in store windows for a while, then bought some milk and some cold meat for lunch and a couple of T-bones to barbecue, if we ever got around to it, at Bert's General Groceries, We Deliver, then passed the rest of the daylight hours in and around the camper, popping in to Tim's from time to time just in case. Sara had brought along a pack of cards so I let her beat me in a couple of games of gin, just to keep her happy, then we both read a bit, Sara some Brautigan rubbish, me a Nero Wolfe I'd already read a half a dozen times, *Fer De Lance*. I knew from the telephone company that when Tommy called the Tavern he always did so around six o'clock, so we were back in the joint well before then, me up front at the bar again and Sara covering the back.

We needn't have bothered, as it turned out, because a few minutes before the hour Tim waved at two men who had just come in and said, 'Hey, Dell, Biff. How you boys doin'?'

'Hangin' in there,' the one who turned out to be Biff said. He came to the bar, picked up a pitcher of beer and two glasses Tim had already set out and took them over to the table where his brother had just sat himself down. After a minute I took a casual look their way. Neither one of the brothers was what you would call young or fresh-faced or innocent, but you wouldn't call them old, scarred villains either. They were just Dell and Biff, two good old redneck boys having a pitcher of suds after work. Dell was the big one, hefty, florid, carrying a few extra pounds around the middle, light brown hair, farmer's jeans, studded leather belt with a flashy Mexican silver buckle depicting the head of a longhorn steer. Biff was short, stocky, in dirty white Levis, old sweater with the sleeves rolled up to show his tattoos, cowboy hat, mirror shades.

Hi, boys, nice to meet you.

'That old jalopy of yours still running?' a young guy in a California Angels baseball cap called out to the brothers from the far end of the bar.

'She just about got us here,' Biff said with a grin, 'but she does tend to buffet a little at high speeds.'

'Uh-huh,' the guy at the bar said, 'Like over forty?'

'Forty?' said Dell. 'I don't even think our speedometer goes that high.' All of which witty repartee led me to suspect that the brothers had something fancy in the form of wheels parked outside, but I needed to know for sure, also I wanted them to get a look at me in my full splendor, i.e., standing up, so I stood up, called to Sara to stay away from the darn phone, I'd be back in a minute, rolled my eyes in the direction of the brothers' table, then headed for the door. I saw the message sink in because she squinted her eyes and called back,

'Make it an hour, who cares.' Then she addressed the room in general, there were maybe ten customers by then, most of whom I'd seen the day before, 'No pool players in here tonight? Shee-it.'

The brothers took a long, careful look at me as I ambled by them, then one at Sara, who was chalking her cue professionally. I don't know where she learned to play the game, but she wasn't bad, although she didn't know anything about position and she loved trying unnecessary bank shots.

'Big mother,' I heard Biff say as I was going out the door.

'Yes indeedy,' his brother said.

Outside, I circled around to the parking area and saw what had to be the brothers' wheels as there was nothing else there of any interest. A new 4 × 4 painted in metallic gold, with a chrome rollbar and four extra spotlights, two mounted on the front of the hood and two more above the driver on the rollbar itself. I was relieved not to see some low-slung Detroit special. I didn't want them changing vehicles on me before they headed into the woods and those bumpy logging roads. I noticed as I passed there was no lock on the gas-tank lid, which was all to the good. Through one of the windows at the back of the tavern I could see both the washrooms and the telephone; after a minute my favorite pool-hustler and birdbrain came out of the ladies' room, stopped at the phone, dug a piece of paper out of her pocket, and started dialing. She was of course calling up the reserves, wherever they were but they wouldn't be far, telling them we'd made contact and it was on for tonight.

Back at the camper I opened up, found the transponder, which was wrapped up in a clean shirt at the bottom of my bag, kissed it for luck, pocketed it, dug out an old, patched cardigan I'd brought along, sat on my bunk for a while just to let a little time pass but not too much, then locked up again and hied it back to the parking lot, swinging the sweater playfully by one sleeve. Wouldn't you know, just as I passed the boys' truck I dropped the damn thing. I couldn't see anyone watching so as I bent to pick it up I whipped off the gas-tank cap, dropped the waterproof (and I devoutly hoped, gasproof) transmitter in, screwed the cap back on, picked up the sweater and continued on my way, hardly having broken stride. I'd never used that kind of transponder before, the kind that went inside the gas tank, the more usual sorts you clamped magnetically under the car in some out-of-the-way spot like beside the exhaust, but those could be found more easily and once in a while fell off. Both types of course had their own power source but as their output was comparatively strong, sending a signal several miles, the batteries only had a working life of some six hours. But that would be more than enough, I prayed, to let us follow at a safe distance an over-dressed 4 × 4, with white leather interior and two large green and white felt dice hanging from the mirror, on its nocturnal travels. White leather interior – hot shit. Sure be a pity if anything happened to that beautiful heap.

Back at Tim's, there had been some changes. Sara, never one to be frightened off by minor character defects like being a killer, was playing eight-ball with Biff. I watched her make a decent long pot but, like I said, she'd left herself no position at all for her next shot. Two cute girls, one of them very cute, who might have been secretaries, if they had such a sophisticated thing in Carmen Springs, had taken the table next to Dell and they were joshing each other in a friendly and well-tried manner. The very cute one took one sidelong glance at me and didn't bother repeating it. I like to think it was the straggly mustache. Biff, however, took a long, hard look at me from the far side of the pool table and he did repeat it. I took that as a good sign; keep looking, Biff – it seemed possible that Sara had already dropped a hint or two that her big, square Daddy wasn't only the amiable goof-off and over-lenient father he was supposed to be.

And things looked even more encouraging when Biff, after putting away the eight-ball with a nice cut into the side pocket, disappeared toward the telephone, then came back, hit Tim for some change, then went back to the phone again. When he went back to his table a minute or two later he looked at everyone but me, then pulled his chair up to Dell's and whispered something to him. Then Dell carefully didn't look at me either.

I had to stick around the place at least til Benny had time to get to the camper and as I was getting peckish I tried another bowl of Tim's chili, which hadn't improved any since the day before, then two hotdogs without, then a sensational pickled wiener for dessert, made, like the pickled eggs, by Tim himself, Maureen the chatty waitress told me as she passed without being asked.

It was right on seven o'clock when Benny appeared, to my shock. In his neat tan outfit, square glasses and black attaché case, short, neatly combed hair and sensible black shoes, he screamed law to me, and I hoped to the brothers as well. We greeted each other with suitable expressions of surprise and pleasure, overdoing it slightly, and when Tim came over to take our drink orders and to take away my empty plates, I introduced him louder than necessary as a friend of mine from LA who'd said he might be up this way and if he was, he'd try and find me by looking in the nearest bar and as Tim's was the only bar in town it hadn't taken him long. We had a good chuckle at that, during which Sara shot us scowls from the brothers' table where she had ensconced herself and where she was helping them finish yet another pitcher of beer.

After we finished our drinks, I paid the bill after a friendly squabble over it with Benny, and we left, not before some undaughterly words from Sara who said she liked it where she was and she was staying where she was until she felt like going somewhere else and wherever that somewhere else was it sure wasn't going to be back to the gross camper that leaked in those boring trees off the parking lot back there by that freezing stream to watch me burn steaks or whatever fun things I had in mind. Not bad for a total nerd; she'd not only got them suspicious of me and my meet with Benny but had even managed to get in the location of the camper and that it was in some trees so it was eminently approachable.

As soon as we were outside I asked Benny why in hell he'd come into the bar. I thought the plan was for him to meet me at the camper.

'I didn't know where it was, did I?' he said mildly. 'Sara talked to Ricky when she phoned. He didn't think to ask and she didn't think to tell him.' And I didn't think to tell her to tell him, I thought.

'Oh, well,' I said. 'She's not used to this sort of thing. Anyone can forget a little detail like that, no harm done.'

'I hope,' said Benny fervently.

As we went by the boys' truck I pointed it out to Benny and told him I'd planted the transmitter with no trouble. He told me Ricky had parked just up the main road but off it, out of sight, and that he had tested the receiver and it was working and he was all ready to move off as soon as the target car hit the road, and also his bird call was working. All right so far. Then Benny and I climbed into the camper to set up the rest of the scam, if I may use that somewhat overworked word.

Overworked or not, it was certainly accurate in our case, for if all went well we were going to scam the brothers Dell and Biff out of their socks, their cowboy boots, their fancy wheels and most, if not all, of their miserable futures.

CHAPTER SEVENTEEN

The first thing I did was to light the gas lamp so there was plenty of interior light, then I opened both side windows a few inches and also carelessly left both side curtains, the adorable gingham ones, half open as well. As the nearest trees were only a few feet away I didn't figure I could make it any easier for Dell or Biff or anyone else, for that matter, who wanted a good eyeful and earful. Then we laid out one of the maps on the fold-down table and scattered a couple of pencils, a ruler and a protractor on top for that professional touch that means so much. I made sure the second receiving set I'd got from Phil, the one that was just an empty box, was in plain view, likewise Benny's briefcase. Then we opened up a beer for me and a soda for Benny and made some small talk as we waited – Benny cool as always, me nervous and getting more so steadily. What we were waiting for was the well-known cry of the red-breasted woodpecker.

We didn't have to wait long before we heard it. It was Ricky, of course, out there in the darkness somewhere, letting us know that we had a customer in place.

'Tell me again, Marshal,' I said stupidly, rubbing my brow, 'I lost you somewhere back there.'

Benny sighed. 'Epilepsy. Also known as grand-mal or petit-mal seizures. Not only does it cause sudden and unpredictable fits of intense energy, it often leaves the sufferer afterwards in a coma from exhaustion. Sometimes there is loss of memory as well. Sometimes there is what is called automatic behavior. It is serious enough in itself, of course, but if it is coupled with, say, diabetes, as it was in the case of Mrs Castillo's brother, it can obviously be fatal. The sufferer could have been lying unconscious for hours after an attack and have died from sugar imbalance.'

'I know all that now,' I said. 'But at first Ricky just told me his brother was, well, slightly mad. He didn't say anything about all this epilepsy and whatnot.' This apparent madness of Chico's was already known by Dell; I had told Ricky to mention it to Tommy and he had passed it on over the phone.

'It is quite usual for relatives to lie about a member of their family having the disease,' Benny pontificated, 'as there has been a great deal of misinformation about it down the ages.'

'Oh,' I said. 'Really.'

Benny took off his glasses and peered through them. 'However, Mr Castillo came up with a rather clever idea. Did he tell you he was in the habit of visiting his brother-in-law at least once a day on his rounds?'

'Absolutely,' I lied.

'Well.' Benny lifted up his briefcase, unlocked it with one of the keys from his keyring and took out a sweat band, the kind of thing tennis players wear around their wrists and wipe their foreheads with all the time. From a small slit in the back of the skin-colored terrycloth band he carefully removed a small black plastic box, which didn't surprise me greatly as I'd put it there the night before. Actually it was a Sen-Sen box I'd painted black with a felt-tip.

'This is a battery-powered transmitter, a common enough type, a similar thing but in reverse to the beepers that doctors wear these days.' And my mom, which had given me the idea in the first place.

'I understand a lot of would-be trendy people wear them too,' I said, 'so they can go beep-beep in public places and make themselves feel important.'

'Our department has found them very useful,' Benny said stiffly. 'I wear one myself in the city.'

'Sorry,' I said meekly.

'This is a spare one Mr Castillo kept in case of emergencies,' Benny went on. 'It doesn't have a large range, slightly over a mile, but that was sufficient for Mr Castillo's purposes. It appears that he once arrived at his brother-in-law's and found him missing. Luckily, he found him some hundred yards away, unconscious, dying from lack of insulin. To prevent that ever happening again, he made him always wear a transmitter like this on his arm under his clothes. If he was for whatever reason going farther away from his base than a mile, he was told to always leave a note saying where he was going and when he expected to be back.'

'I know that, that's how I knew he was heading up here to pot paradise,' I said mendaciously, not really wanting to advertise to the likes of Dell and Biff let alone anyone else that I had illegally bugged Tommy's home.

'Now,' said Benny, tapping the ruler against the map in a fussy manner. 'May I draw your attention to the northern sector of the Forestry Commission land, roughly, here. You will note that the terrain is irregular but fairly comprehensively criss-crossed by a grid of service and logging roads. I made an approximate calculation and estimated that over three quarters of the area in question is within a mile of a road of some kind, so if we cover them all we stand a good chance of locating the poor man. I'm afraid that our medical examiner told me that after all this time there is very little chance of finding him alive, but stranger things have happened. At least he can be pronounced legally dead and we can take his body back to his family for a decent Christian burial.'

He took off his glasses again to peer fruitlessly through them. 'I personally wouldn't mind if my tired old bones rested here for ever among the green trees and fresh air, but . . .'

I stopped his ad-libbing before it got out of hand by murmuring, 'Quite, quite. And we track him with this?' I patted the top of the receiving set.

'Indeed,' said Benny. 'There is a smaller version but as we'll be in a car we might as well have the more powerful model that doesn't depend on line of sight to pick up a signal.'

'Meaning it works through hills,' I said.

'Obviously,' he said. This was to take away any hope our eavesdropper might have that if the signal was coming from six feet under it would be undetectable.

'Fascinating,' I said. 'I've never seen a model like this before. I've really got to try and keep up with things.'

'There's no sense wandering around those awful roads tonight,' Benny said. 'Especially as, unfortunately, the poor chap is almost certainly dead by now. Why don't you get a good night's sleep and I'll come by tomorrow morning at a reasonable hour, say about six?'

'I don't call that reasonable,' I said, 'but OK, if you say so, sir. I am bushed, I must admit. I think it's all this fresh air.' I even managed to yawn. I snuck a look at my friend Benny who had not only learned his lines but had stayed in character throughout so brilliantly I almost believed what he was saying. All in all, I was proud of my troops and, without being sickening about it, pleased with myself. We had managed to cover all the bases so far. We had maneuvered at least one of the brothers in position and fed him the bait and would soon know if he ran with it. We couldn't let on that we suspected Chico had been murdered, because there wasn't supposed to be any way we could know that. More importantly, there wasn't much point in letting the brothers know ahead of time we suspected them, God knows what they might do, burn down the whole forest, hop a plane to Pago Pago, kill us all. I wanted to leave them an out, an easy out that involved moving Chico's body. As it stood, we'd established, I hoped, that we could find him if he was anywhere within a mile of a road, and the odds were overwhelming that he was, as why would Biff and Dell lug a dead body more than a mile through the woods when they could go a hundred yards off the road in any one of a thousand places, dig a hole, dump him in, and he'd never be seen again.

Now it looked like they would have to lug the body a mile or two, but no real problem, there wasn't much to him, pobre Chico, they could get the whole thing done in a couple of hours and be back at Tim's playing pool and laughing at us and the world by ten o'clock.

So they thought. So I hoped they thought.

We had to wait for the woodpecker to sound the all-clear, so I asked Benny if he would care for a nightcap before he left. He said primly he'd already had his alcoholic consumption for the day, thank you, referring to the one small beer he'd drunk half of at Tim's earlier, but he admitted he wouldn't mind another soda pop if I had a sugar-free one. I said I didn't. Then he asked me if I happened to have any cocoa. I said I didn't have any of that either. Before he asked me for some other foolish beverage I didn't have, like sassafras tea, Ricky the woodpecker crowed, or trilled, which meant it was time to move.

I grabbed my navy-blue windbreaker and Sara's knapsack, which I had earlier requisitioned and prepacked with the .38, loaded, in a shoulder holster, the box of cartridges, flashlight, blunt instrument, handcuffs, the camera and the flares and a few other odds and ends we might never need but just in case.

'You watch the store,' I told Benny as I climbed out.

'Forget it, Uncle,' he said, rummaging in his briefcase. 'Include me in.' He came up with a little ladies' automatic about three inches long and slipped it in a pocket.

'Jesus,' I said, 'where did you get that?'

'Borrowed it.'

'From who, Mata Hari?'

'My sister,' he said. Then he dug out a flashlight, a foot-long sheath knife and a bottle of insect repellent. Brilliant;

even I knew you didn't get mosquitoes in January. However, there wasn't any time to argue with him, not that it would have done any good because arguing with Benny was like arguing with General Patton – whatever happened, you lost – so I made him put on a dark sweater of mine, then I locked up and we hurried out to the main road by way of the unlit side of Tim's parking lot.

'Where's the hell's Ricky?' I asked Benny a few minutes later as we were trotting along.

'Not far,' he said, puffing a bit. 'Off the road just around the next bend. I hope it's the next bend. I haven't run this far since summer camp.'

A minute later a car pulled out of a side road right in front of us; it was Ricky in the Jeep. He spotted us, pulled over, and stopped. I hopped in the front with him and Benny fell in the back. Ricky was all in dark clothes too, his all-purpose belt already around his waist. He made a smart U-turn and headed west, on the road we'd originally taken into Carmen Springs but going in the opposite direction.

'This thing working?' I asked Ricky, referring to the receiving set which was on the floor by my feet.

He nodded. 'Maps on the seat beside you,' he said to Benny.

'How do we know which way they went?' I wondered out loud, as the receiver couldn't tell you what direction the signal came from, only its strength.

'I saw them go by,' Ricky said.

'How did you know it was them?'

'Sara told me on the phone they had this half-ton all loaded with extra crap and small-town shit.'

'How did she know?'

'She said she saw you out the window being furtive right beside it.'

'Oh God,' I said. 'I hope no one else saw me.'

'Nope,' said Ricky, shaking his head. 'She said that's what

she was doing at the window in the first place, making sure no one else was looking out.'

'Well,' I said, 'score another one for the noodlehead.'

'Maybe you should keep your mind on your work,' Benny put in from the back seat. 'As I understand it if we get too close to those guys and they suddenly pull up and kill their motor, they could hear us coming. And if we get too far behind them we might miss them turning off.'

'Aren't you supposed to be map-reading?' I said. I fiddled with the dials of the receiver a bit and almost immediately had a steady humming signal coming in. I saw from the visual read-out they were getting away from us so I asked Ricky to speed up a little. He put his foot down.

'How many feet in half a mile?' I asked the troops after a while, because I figured that would be a sensible distance to keep between us.

'A lot,' said Benny.

'Two thousand six hundred and forty,' said Ricky. I took his word for it.

'Slow down a bit,' I told him. He obliged.

It is not easy following another vehicle at night, at a distance, on unknown roads. One big advantage we had over the first leg was we knew they were heading back to forestry land and there was only one direct way to get there, which Ricky had thoughtfully penciled in on the map Benny was fumbling with. What would happen after, though, when we turned off on to one of those miserable logging roads, would be in the lap of the gods. When I mentioned this to my brave boys, Ricky shook his head again and said,

'No hay problema. It rained last night, remember?'

I remembered all right. It was lucky I hadn't caught pneumonia.

'So what?' asked Benny.

'So tracks,' I said. 'Nice new tracks in the mud.'

We drove on steadily through the night, keeping our distance, thinking our thoughts. A half moon appeared to keep us company. We almost lost the boys once when they took a back road we hadn't counted on but we picked them up after a moment of controlled panic and closed in to a half mile again.

It was forty minutes til they turned off into forestry land, right where Ricky had marked it on the map. He switched off our headlights and we began slowly bumping our way through the trees. We didn't seem to be falling any further behind so we figured the boys had slowed down and were driving without lights too. I kept my eyes firmly on the dial but it was another twenty minutes before I noticed that although we were creeping along at the same speed, the distance between us was shortening steadily.

'OK,' I told Ricky. 'I think that's it. Shut off the motor for a minute, will you?'

He switched off the ignition key. Only the wind in the treetops and the occasional ping from the cooling engine broke the silence. 'Let's move it,' I said quietly. 'We want to catch the bastards in the act. We don't want to have to trail them miles through the jungle.' I got my gun out of the knapsack and strapped it on.

'Right on,' said Benny. We got out of the Jeep as quietly as we could, leaving the doors open rather than trying to close them without making any noise.

'When we get there,' I whispered, 'Ricky, you go all the way around them and close in from the far side. Benny, I'll head left, you go right. It'll take you longest to get into position, Ricky, so when you do, make like a bird again. Then we all hit them with the flashlights at the same time from three different directions and for Christ's sake hold the lights away from your body just in case. Ricky, all that hardware on your belt, it's not going to clank together and sound like the cows are coming home, is it?'

Ricky checked and moved a couple of items farther apart,

then we took off in single file up the logging road, Ricky leading, then Benny, then me. We tried to make as much time as we could but the going was uneven, muddy, slippery, dark under the trees and downright treacherous. Both Benny and I stumbled into the muck a few times but Ricky seemed to manage somehow.

It was an unpleasant twenty-five minutes later when Ricky whispered back, 'Truck up ahead.'

When we got to it, Benny and I crouched down beside it getting our wind back while Ricky had a quick look around. He was back in a minute and crouched down with us.

'Light,' he whispered, pointing off into the trees. I couldn't see any bloody light from where I was but when we got some ten yards into the woods, stepping as carefully as we could, I did see the occasional flicker through the underbrush and after another twenty or thirty yards heard the unmistakable sounds of someone digging.

Ricky pressed my arm then began moving off to the left in a wide circle to get behind them. Benny and I gave him a few minutes, then we started edging our way closer. Luckily for us tenderfoots, we were walking over a sound-deadening carpet of wet pine needles. We closed in to within twenty feet of the light, always keeping a tree trunk between us and them, then I poked my head extremely cautiously around a deadfall that was propped up at an angle and there they were, the good old boys themselves, Biff digging with a short-handled spade and his brother keeping his light steady on the deepening hole.

I pulled back, tapped Benny on the arm, and gestured off to the right. He nodded, made a thumb's-up gesture, and started edging away. I sneaked over to the left some ten yards then took another peek. The brothers had changed places by then, Dell was up to his knees in the hole digging and Biff was holding the light on him. Biff took a bottle of some kind of booze out of his back pocket and took a long swallow. His brother said something to him I couldn't hear. Then I noticed Dell had a long-barreled revolver tucked in his belt. I got my own gun out, got the flash ready, and crouched there, waiting, trying not too successfully to keep my breathing quiet, deep, and steady. Well, you don't go to war every day.

I waited. Dell cursed once. I waited some more. Then Dell said, 'Got him.'

'Thank fuck,' said his brother.

Then the woodpecker sounded its mating call. Our three flashlights came on all at the same time. I was holding mine on one side of the tree trunk and looking around the other side. I had the .38 resting against the damp bark keeping it steady and had a bead on the center of Dell's chest.

'Freeze!' I shouted. 'Police! You're surrounded by armed troops! Move and you will be shot!'

Dell froze. Biff didn't. We, or more honestly, I, had forgotten one thing – to decide who was supposed to shine his light on who. Of course what happened was all three of us were covering Dell. Biff dropped his light and disappeared into the blackness.

'Ricky, stay with the guy in the hole!' I shouted, getting my brain working a little late. 'You others, find that mother!' But before Benny or I could pick up Biff, he had picked up a pump shotgun from somewhere and he let fly in my direction. The second shot got my right arm, which was still holding the flashlight; thank God most of the load either hit the tree trunk or went wide. I was more surprised than anything, it didn't even hurt for a few moments. Then I saw Benny's light luckily catch one of Biff's legs, which was sticking out from behind a tree. His little pop gun went, pop, pop, twice, I could see the double spurt of material in Biff's trousers, right at the knee, and he went down swearing. Dell still hadn't budged an inch, which was just as well for him, because the state Ricky was in, he only needed the slightest excuse to let him have it.

I shouted to the troops, 'Move in, and keep your lights on

the bastards.' I ran to where Biff was groaning and holding his leg, hauled him up, dragged him a few feet to a tree and cuffed his hands behind it. I tossed Benny the other pair of cuffs and he did the same to Dell after easing his gun from his belt, while Ricky kept his machete pressed up against Dell's throat just in case he got any bright ideas. Then Ricky went over to the grave, stepped in, and began throwing out handfuls of dirt. After a minute, Biff ran out of breath and stopped swearing. After another minute, my arm started throbbing, then burning. After another minute, Ricky said softly,

'It's him.' Benny and I went over and looked down. Pobre Chico looked up at us with dirt-filled eyes. Ricky scooped out a few more handfuls of earth until he disclosed a jagged hole in Chico's upper chest.

'Entry wound,' said Ricky.

'Yeah,' I said. 'Be nice if there's no exit wound and the bullet's still in there and even nicer if it comes from that asshole's .38 that Benny's still waving around.'

'Hey, man, my brother,' the asshole in question called over to us. 'He's dying, baby.'

'No such luck,' I said. 'Ricky, come out of there, there's nothing more to do there.' I gave him a hand up.

He noticed my torn sleeve and asked me what happened.

'Lucky bugger got me with some birdshot,' I said.

'It wasn't birdshot, mother-fucker,' said Dell. 'It was double O.'

I went over and kicked him in the head.

'Speak when you're spoken to,' I said. Then I said to my brave boys, 'Follow me, lads.' We withdrew some few yards into the trees where we couldn't be overheard.

'You gonna leave us here, cunt-face?' Dell shouted after us.

'Not a bad idea,' said Benny thoughtfully. 'You all right, Uncle?'

'Yeah, thanks to you and that sissy gun of yours,' I said. 'I never even knew you could shoot.'

'I've only done it twice,' said Benny. 'How about you, Ricky, how you doing?'

'Terrific,' said Ricky with a grin. 'We got the coños, no?'

'We sure did,' said Benny. 'What a night. Let's do it again sometime, like in a hundred years.'

'I hate to break up the party,' I said, 'but we got things to do. Ricky, you got two minutes to find out from the hermanos where their plantation is. I don't care how you do it as long as you don't kill them. Ask them about mines and boobytraps, too.'

'Con mucho gusto,' said Ricky, with a wide smile. He went off and Benny took a closer look at my arm under the light of his flash. Together we counted eight puckers where pellets were embedded but there was just a trickle of blood from a few of them and nothing from the rest.

'Soon have them out,' my friend said.

'Sooner the better,' I said. 'Be just like those fuckers to have rubbed all their shot in garlic or curare.'

Ricky came silently back through the trees.

'That was quick,' I said.

'And quiet, too,' Benny said.

'I found a rock,' Ricky said. 'More like a small boulder. I could just about lift it. I told the big one I'd drop it on his brother's knee. He told me the plantation is only a mile and a half from here and how to get to it.'

'Boobytraps?'

'No mines,' Ricky said. 'A couple of grenades attached to fishing line.'

'Well, get going, but be careful,' I said. 'Then get back to Tim's. Benny, you and Sara take off in the camper. I want you both out of here. Take the receiver from the Jeep, too, and anything else that looks suspicious. Then and only then, Ricky, you call the cops and an ambulance and bring them back here. I'll hang around and keep an eye on the boys until you do. The last thing we need now is for them to spring those cheap cuffs and take off. OK? Vamoose, amigos. See you back in town, Benny. Ta ta to Sara. Oh. Do me a favor, on your way do something nasty and permanent to the boys' fancy wheels.'

They vamoosed. I went back to the brothers, helped myself to Biff's bottle, which was luckily still intact and which turned out to be Wild Turkey, and, as I had a while to wait, made myself more or less comfortable sitting on a bed of needles, resting my back against a handy tree. I kept the flash on all the time, alternating it between the two, sipping the bourbon and thinking clean thoughts.

About ten minutes later there was the muffled thump of a minor explosion from the direction of the logging road, then a brief burst of flame.

'What the fuck was that?' Dell wanted to know.

'It sounded like someone tossed a match in a gas tank,' I said. 'Probably kids. Lucky for them the woods are wet so there's no chance of the fire spreading.'

'Yeah, real lucky,' said Dell.

And that was it as far as conversation went for the next two hours and twenty minutes. Biff had passed out and Dell had finally realized it might be smarter to keep his mouth shut, so he did. And that was fine by me. I listened to the wind in the treetops and the friendly gurgle of good bourbon sliding down an appreciative throat and watched the stars come out to play. My arm burned and sizzled for a while, then stopped.

All too soon, almost, in a strange way, there were lights, sirens, cameras, action. There were sheriff's men, an ambulance, a portable lab, a dog handler and God knows what other backup forces just waiting for a call. A male nurse with a heavy beard called Cyril gave me a local anesthetic and laboriously dug out nine, it turned out, pieces of shot from my arm. Cyril wanted to know if I wanted to keep them as a souvenir.

'No thanks, Cyril,' I said. 'I'd rather keep my arm.'

CHAPTER EIGHTEEN

Ricky and I spent most of Wednesday in and around Carmen Springs doing what we had done the night before until five thirty – answering questions. Well, answering the ones we could without making even more trouble for ourselves.

We had prepared a fallback position designed to protect ourselves as much as possible but especially to protect him; if it came out that he had been feeding and giving shelter to an illegal alien on government property, the least of his problems would be finding a new job. He might blow any pension he had accumulated and of course his free medical. So we'd come up with the following:

Some time ago, a Mr Lupinez (name chosen at random), biologist and naturalist, had applied to Ricky for official permission to make wildlife studies in forestry land. (Samples of his work on request.) In view of the department's official policy of maintaining good relations with the public, limited permission had been granted, in writing, by Ricky. (A copy of said permission to be produced by Ricky as soon as he had typed one out, pre-dated it, and signed it.) Mr Lupinez's credentials, now unfortunately no longer to be found, seemed to be completely authentic. Mr Lupinez had informed Ricky early in January of his discovery of illegal activities taking place on forestry land, to wit, the growing of illicit substances, to wit, weed, and a lot of it. Suspecting that a fellow officer of the Forestry Service, who was also a friend, might be involved, and thus not wanting to call in official aid unless and until it was absolutely necessary, Ricky had asked one V. Daniel, an old acquaintance and skilled investigator, for his assistance, which had been freely given, V. Daniel being the good citizen he was.

Their investigations had led them to Carmen Springs, where the suspicious behavior of Dell and Biff (family name Redman, it turned out) had attracted their attention. During a routine surveillance, the investigators had discovered to their surprise and horror the brothers digging up a body that turned out to be that of Mr Lupinez. The gunfight that followed was described to investigating officers from the Sheriff's Department as it happened, except that I took the credit for shooting Biff, to get Benny off the hook.

So that was our simple story, and we planned to stick with it up to and including the trial, whenever that would be. We didn't think anyone would believe for a moment any foolish ramblings the brothers might make about epilepsy and brothers-in-law and electronic experts and beepers and punk daughters. And anyway, not being completely stupid, the brothers would probably refuse to say anything at all because there was nothing that they could say that would help. And when Ricky was questioned for more details about his friend and fellow officer who might be involved, he merely said politely that he would be able to give a fuller statement the following day after he'd had a chance to speak with his superiors. And what that did was to give me a day to set up Tommy DeMarco, because if he and the boys did keep their mouths shut, he was free and clear.

The boys, of course, had had it. One murder count, because even if the law couldn't match up the bullet that killed Chico with Dell's gun, the boys would have a fairly difficult time explaining what they were doing digging up a corpse in the middle of the night in the woods; how did they know it was there if they hadn't put it there? And why would they put it there if they were innocent? And in California, as in many states, if a murder is committed during the course of a felony, all parties to the felony are considered party to the murder, double something it is called. See, reading does pay off. They also had an attempted murder rap against them – mine. Also, it was odds on Dell's hand gun wasn't licensed. And how about illegal possession of little items like hand grenades and who knew what else? Let alone the Garden of Eden.

The boys in blue and various other colors finally let us go that evening after we'd signed innumerable statements and promised we wouldn't leave the country without letting them know, and we also swore we would be available for the trial if called. Then we had to deal with a swarm of reporters who jumped us at Tim's when I popped in to say goodbye; I said I was sworn to secrecy, had one for the road, and we took off, Ricky driving, in the Jeep.

I had a thought on the way home.

'Remember those groceries Tommy gave you?'

'Sure,' Ricky said. 'Still haven't touched the ham.'

'What about the carton, would that still be around?'

'Knowing Ellena, it is,' he said.

'Want to drop it around to my office tomorrow morning?'

'Sure,' he said. 'Handling it carefully, I presume.'

'You presume correctly,' I said. We didn't say much during the rest of the drive, but once in a while would look at each other and laugh.

Getting home was a solid pleasure. I didn't bother to unpack the camper, which was parked out front waiting for me, I went straight up to the apartment, opened up a couple of windows, had a soak in the tub, made myself somewhat clumsily two baloney sandwiches and took them and a glass of buttermilk and myself to bed. I called up Mom and had a word with her. Then I phoned Evonne and had a lot of words with her, including a few, but not all, lovey-dovey ones. The ones that weren't lovey-dovey covered the old familiar territory, why didn't I ever tell her exactly what I was doing and how come she never met any of my friends, she introduced me to all her friends. Then I took two Mogadons and went to sleep.

*

Thursday, 22 Jan. (I am tempted to put the remainder of this account in free verse, but good taste prevents me.) At the office. Arm in an eye-catching sling made from one of Mom's 'Souvenir of Oahu' scarves. Called the messsage service to demand the instant appearance of Willing Boy. The girl said he'd be here in a jiff. Called Parson's Crossing and ascertained without arousing suspicion that Tommy had showed up for work and was out in the field. Called a sleepy Benny and told him to expect Willing Boy in the next half hour and to please have the package ready for him. Had a quick visit from Ricky, who gingerly handed me the vegetable carton, shook hands, then left. Had a coffee next door. Came back to find Gorgeous sprawling in my visitor's chair. Sent him over to Benny's. Checked the mail – there was one inquiry about my fees from a lawyer in Century City that looked promising and several bills, including one from Wade, that didn't.

When Gorgeous returned he had ten Ks of the boys' home grown in a shopping bag tucked under his arm, although I hoped he didn't know it. I sent him for a walk while I re-packed the weed into the carton, then threw in for good measure a rusty but still serviceable Remington .25 I'd come across in my travels and put away in the safe for a rainy day and also as an extra added bonus I chucked in four glassine envelopes of heroin, part of the stash I'd found in Dev Devlin's kitchen the year before. All right. That should take care of Tommy's social life for a while, say, one to three.

I phoned Tommy's house to make sure no one, like a cleaning lady, was in. No one was. I put my head out the door and whistled for Gorgeous, who was leaning against a tree watching the girls go by. I reminded him of Tommy's address, gave him the package, told him to handle it with much care, and then when he found there was no one home, to leave the carton in the garage, which Sara had told me in one of her loony reports wasn't kept locked.

'When you have finished your little chore, you might be

kind enough to telephone me and tell me so,' I said. 'Got a dime?'

'I do,' he said. 'Do not worry, Chief, have I ever failed you?'

We settled on a fee and off he went. About half an hour later he called in to report that all had gone smoothly and that the carton was now safely stowed under a workbench at the rear of the garage. Not only hadn't he seen anyone remotely interested in him, he hadn't seen anyone at all, which was a Good Thing. I know I've done it before, planted evidence, and I'll do it again, often the old tricks are the best ones, as the actress said to the octogenarian. And I didn't like Tommy. He was fresh-faced, young and good-looking. I suppose there were other reasons.

Then I put in a call to my favorite midget policeman, one Lieutenant Conyers, a pint-sized clothes horse who'd been around during the previously mentioned Dev Devlin affair and who worked out of L A P D Central. As he was not only a policeman working out of Narcotics but had an only son who was, or who had been back then, a hop-head, his position on drug peddlers was somewhere to the extreme right of J. Edgar Hoover's.

Lieutenant Conyers was in.

'This is a well-meaning citizen who wants to remain nameless, Tiny,' I said.

'Oh, Christ,' he said. 'You again.'

'Please!' I said. 'No names. If you want a nice substantial drug bust, listen closely.' I gave him Tommy's name and address. I knew the lieutenant couldn't legally enter a premise without either a warrant or due cause, so I gave him a due cause: not only was I a nameless, well-meaning citizen but I was a nameless close neighbor of Mr DeMarco's and I had seen suspicious activities in his garage a couple of nights before, activities centering around a medium-sized cardboard box.

He sighed heavily.

'Sure you did,' he said.

'You might also check with the phone company about any calls he's made to a number up north in dear old Carmen Springs,' I said, and gave him the number of Tim's Tavern. 'I have information that he has been in regular contact with two brothers from up there who were arrested yesterday on about a thousand counts, including one murder, that of a Mr Lupinez, and one attempted murder, that of a brave and selfless investigator from down here in the Valley somewhere.'

'Anything else?'

'I'd check the box for fingerprints, if I were you, thank God I'm not.'

'Sounds familiar,' he said. 'Anything else?'

'You might say thanks,' I said, 'if your Napoleon complex will let you thank a man twice your size. Or is it three times?'

'Up yours,' he said, and hung up.

Friday, 23 Jan. Took Evonne to meet one of my close friends – Harry, the night barman over at the Three Jacks.

Saturday, 24 Jan. Received, at the office, delivered by hand, yet another lengthy report from Agent S. S., punk detective, covering our recent adventures up north in timber-wolf country. I will quote only one line here: 'Wonderful trip back to L A with Agent B. (name on request). Sang the whole time.' I'm not surprised, with at least ten kilos of grade-A sinsemilla riding unprotected with them.

Monday, 26 Jan. Chico's body was released by the coroner's office to one Enrique Castillo, as no one of the deceased's family had come forth to claim it. Later that day he, his wife and myself attended a mercifully brief ceremony, if that's the word, at the Peterson Bros Funeral Home, down in Inglewood not far from the Castillos' home. The three of us sat in folding chairs listening to recorded organ music for a while, trying not to look at the coffin which was on a long table to our right. When I finally did look over at it, it was eerily moving down the table until it disappeared through a curtained opening. Fifteen minutes later, in the anteroom out front, an attendant handed Ricky a clay urn containing all that was left of pobre Chico.

And later still that day, Ricky and I retraced our footsteps one last time out past Parson's Crossing and through the woods to Chico's cabin, now empty and stripped of all traces of Chico by Ricky on his return from Carmen Springs, as I had suggested. Ricky had brought along one of those collapsible entrenching tools you often see in the windows of war surplus stores and with it, just at sunset, he dug a hole and put in the urn of ashes, then filled in the hole again. Then Ricky quietly said something in Spanish while I quietly thought something in English. Then we went home.

Tuesday, 27 Jan. At the office. For want of anything to do I was leafing through the local rag, a weekly that came out every Friday, to see if my small but discreet ad had been published, one that I had paid for in advance. I found it; it looked quite impressive, I thought, tucked in there under 'Services' between 'Madame Clara – Clairvoyante – In The Privacy Of Your Own Abode' and a two-line ad for a school of dentistry.

The paper had strictly local news, if news is the right word for bowling league results and scoops like 'J. D. Armstrudder, Vice-President of Oswego Metals, Ltd, was the guest speaker at Wednesday's Rotary Luncheon held as usual in the Admiral's Room of the La Salle Hotel. "Jake" Armstrudder gave a forceful address on the topic, "Muddled Thinking in Middle Management".'

There were also the usual lists of local church services, the police report, all the garage sales in the neighborhood and a short list of people who were 'In' or 'Out', meaning in or out of hospital, and in the 'In' column there was the name of Mrs Kevin Donovan, whom I had completely forgotten. So I locked up and walked the few blocks over to the Palmettos, guilty as a small boy with a new BB gun who has just taken a highly forbidden snap shot at a bird and actually hit and killed it.

I went up to the second floor and knocked on the Donovan door. After a few moments it was opened by old hole in one himself. He was wearing an apron and was holding in one hand, his left hand, I noticed, one of those squeegie things on a stick with which people wash floors.

'Hi, pal,' I said coldly. 'Remember me, or are you the new au pair?'

He looked at me through pale blue eyes, then turned away without saying anything and plodded back down the hall. I followed him. When I caught up with him he was washing the kitchen floor from a plastic bucket full of soapy water.

'I saw your wife was in the hospital,' I said, leaning against the door jamb. 'Read it in the paper.'

He still didn't say anything but went on methodically going over and over a patch of linoleum that already looked clean to me. Maybe it was displacement activity. Maybe it was penance. Maybe it was role reversal. Maybe it was just something to do between drinks.

'What did you do to her this time,' I said after another while, 'hit her with a sand wedge?'

Silence. Well, what did he have to say, anyway? For that matter, what did I? I watched him for a few more minutes, then said, 'So long, keep your head down,' and headed for the front door. As soon as I closed it behind me, I heard him start to sing 'The Rose of Tralee'. You figure it out.

Two weeks later Benny phoned to tell me it looked like the gold deal was going to happen, so I called Mr Lubinski at his brother's back East in freezing Philly and told him the good news, that it looked like he was off the hook.

'What kept you?' he wanted to know.

And one week after that Lubinski, Lubinski and Levi celebrated its reopening with a small after-hours party at the store for a few selected guests. It was a catered affair.

I'd seen the girl who was bartending at similar affairs in the neighborhood before. She was a pretty, not so young anymore actress between engagements, as they say in her profession. Good luck, they say in mine. Poor old thespians, if they're not up to their hips in waterfalls or acting as bear meat, they're pouring drinks for the likes of me and my friends.

Having taken to heart, or at least pretended to, Evonne's recent comments about a certain thoughtlessness in my behavior in certain areas, I had invited a considerable number of my close friends for her to finally meet. It served her right, was what I thought about it. Benny was there, in a dark-blue double-breasted number I'd never seen before. Elroy my office landlord and millionaire was there in his usual garb of wraparound shades, disgraceful jeans, ragged T-shirt and torn flip-flops. J.D., ex-pro bowler and proud prop of the Valley Bowl was there, handsome as all get out in his Valley leisure wear. Wade and Suze were there, smashed out of their skulls and devouring everything in sight including the cream-cheese-filled celery sticks. My mom was there, tossing back a Manhattan cocktail and chatting animatedly with Mrs Martel from across the street. Ricky was there, in a white tropical suit, but Ellena had stayed home as she was going through a queasy period in her pregnancy. Jim the barman from the Two-Two-Two was there, I'd never seen him in a suit before, but Harry from the Three Jacks was working that night. I'd somehow forgotten to invite my brother.

Olivia the llama-lover was there, so was Emile Douglas,

the one who chatted to God. They were at the rear of the store chatting together about something vulgar like cross-breeding. And of course Mr Lubinski and Mr Lubinski were there with their wives, also several friends of theirs, plus a quiet, well-dressed elderly gentleman whom nobody seemed to know but who nodded politely in my direction from time to time. Oh, I forgot Mr Lowenstein, Evonne's boss, and his wife Ethyl. Needless to say, Evonne, my sweetheart, was there as well, elegant in basic black and high heels with a black bandeau around her curls. And, finally, also needless to say, Ms Sara Silvetti, poetess and nerd extraordinaire, had condescended to attend. She was, for her, modestly attired in a tatty lace nightgown worn over a flesh-colored body stocking, with contrasting accessories – a tin lunch pail as a purse and one elbow-length black evening glove. To complete the ensemble, around her slim neck hung a huge lei made of plastic flowers.

After a pleasant hour of imbibing, mingling, introducing, imbibing and munching, Mr Lubinski took me aside, told me how much he liked my friends – funny, Evonne had said the same thing – told me how much he'd hated Philadelphia, his brother Mort and their three spoiled brats, asked me what I thought of the new necklace his wife was wearing, then asked me, 'Got a watch?'

'Sure I got a watch,' I said. 'Everyone's got a watch.' I showed him mine with some pride. It was a beauty I'd been given last Christmas.

'That's a watch?' he said scornfully. 'That's a watch I buy for sixteen dollars wholesale and sell in this store to tourists for forty-nine fifty. Who gave you that, an enemy?'

'No, a landlord,' I said, giving Elroy a dirty look.

'Here,' Mr Lubinski said, taking a jeweler's box out of his pocket and pressing it into my hands. 'Now you got a watch. Enjoy.' He slapped me on the back and moved away.

I opened the box and, like he said, now I had a watch. Slim

as a philanderer's alibi, heavy as a broken heart. It didn't tell you the phases of the moon or do your income tax or tell you what time it was somewhere you didn't care about anyway, like Singapore, or wake you up with a snooze alarm. All it did was tell you what time it was in Los Angeles, California, and tell everyone else who saw it that under your frayed cuff you had a timepiece worth more than their family car. I hoped he wouldn't want it back when he got my bill.

I looked around for Evonne so I could show it to her but I spotted Sara first and that reminded me of something so I took her by one bony arm and led her out back, past Olivia and Emile, where I'd left a large box on a table when I'd first come in.

'Got a typewriter?' I asked her.

'Sure I got a typewriter,' she said. 'Everyone's got a type-writer. It's a wreck but it works.'

'Now you got a typewriter,' I said, gesturing eloquently towards the box. She gave me a disbelieving look, but opened up the carton. In it was one of those new Canons, the expensive ones, with the screen that lets you see a whole line before you enter it. It might have even had some memory capacity, how would I know. She stared at it, then jumped up and grabbed me around the neck and hung on, like I was some kind of tree.

'All right, all right,' I said. 'Don't crease your jeans.'

'All right yourself,' she said, untangling herself. Then she looked at me suspiciously. 'What's come over you all of a sudden? Win the lottery?'

'Oh, just a whim,' I said bashfully, scuffing my feet a bit. I didn't bother telling her where the money for her sensational and unexpected present had come from. Why should I, it was none of her Nosey Parker business. Even I wasn't supposed to know, officially, but I managed to figure it out. It was part of, let us say, a tenth of a check which Benny had mailed me a few days earlier. He claimed, nay, he swore til he was blue in the face that the money was a finder's fee for me setting him up with the gold deal, but I had my suspicions. I deeply suspected that when I sent him and Ricky to the plantation to lift a few Ks to frame Tommy with if we had to, those two had loaded up the Jeep with all the prime weed they could find, switched it to the camper, then Benny had peddled it for top dollar back in LA, no doubt paying off that pot-head Sara with a lid or two to keep her quiet.

But what could I prove? Also, if I kept Benny's check, it meant that I could give Ellena's check back to her, which I had already done, knowing how expensive new babies are. I really don't see I had any choice in the matter.

But that wasn't the last of the gift-giving. When I got back into the main room, the quiet, elderly gentleman whom nobody seemed to know, who had watched approvingly as Mr Lubinski had presented me with my new watch, came up to me and said, 'Excuse me, Mr Victor Daniel?'

'Right on,' I said. 'I don't believe I got your name.'

'Tony Garden,' he said with a gentle smile. 'I believe you know a business associate of mine.'

'Well, I haven't actually met him but I've heard a lot of good things about him,' I said. 'How do you know who I am?'

'Tsk, tsk,' he said, and gave another little laugh. So did I. Mine was deeply forced.

'You should be in my line of business,' I said.

'I'll take that as a compliment,' he said.

'It was certainly intended as one,' I said cravenly, hoping he wouldn't smile again because the more he smiled the less I liked it.

'By the way, I have a present for you too,' he said. 'And for Mr Lubinski. And for your friend Benjamin.'

'You really shouldn't have,' I said. 'I hope it's nothing extravagant, like half of Las Vegas.'

'Better,' he said. 'Peace of mind.' He smiled. 'For now.' He headed for the door. I headed for the bar.

Evonne took one look at me and said, 'You all right?'

'For now,' I said. 'Bartender, a brandy and ginger. Make it a double.'

Five weeks later Ellena was delivered of a baby, weight six pounds six ounces. For some reason, the proud parents named it after me – Victoria.

Well, close enough.